THE POSTHUMOUS MAN
JAKE HINKSON

Cover by Michael Kronenberg.

ISBN: 978-0-9912039-2-5

www.beattoapulp.com

Contents

For Heather,
Who dwells in Possibility.

In a murderous time
  the heart breaks and breaks
    and lives by breaking.
It is necessary to go
  through dark and deeper dark
    and not to turn.

From Stanley Kunitz's "The Testing-Tree"

In My Moment of Dying   1

From the darkness, something stabbed through my face.

I tried to grab it, tried pull it out, but I couldn't find it. A woman shouted, "His arm is loose—"

A hard red light sheared the top off the darkness and peeled it back like skin. Far above me, a red hole opened.

I tried to say something, but my body didn't seem connected. I couldn't see, couldn't hear clearly, couldn't make my arms work. I was conscious of movement around me, flickers of light and speech, but I couldn't find my voice.

The red light got brighter, closer, and dark blobs darted in front of it. The blackness shook around me.

A man barked out, "Is that endotrach—"

They shoved the tube through my face and down my throat. I gagged, tried to get at it again, rip it out.

"Loose—"

"For God's sake, restrain his arm correc—"

I got hold of the tube and yanked on it. Above me the red light swelled and brightened, pressing down and pushing against my eyelids. The center of the light burned white.

"Restrain that goddamn arm," someone yelled.

I ripped the tube out and my eyes popped open. Masked figures in green crowded around me. Above them a huge white lamp beat down like a cold winter sun. I tasted plastic and vomit and blood. Gloved hands stinking with the dry smell of latex worked just above my face.

The hands moved away, and I saw her.

A nurse, her face worried and concentrated on saving my life, stood over me, and her blue eyes lifted for an instant and met mine. She blinked and raised a hand toward my face. On her pale wrist I saw a perfect black star. I grabbed the star, but they strapped my arm down and somebody shoved the tube up my nose again.

"We're losing him—"

I gagged and my vision yellowed and bubbled over. The nurse drifted away.

My whole body plunged, like a stone dropping to the bottom of a well. Soft, painless black welcomed me. I slowed, floating downward now, the blackness spreading up to the top of my pit and choking the light.

The white circle at the top got smaller and smaller, until it was only a pinpoint.

Then the blackness sealed shut.

* * *

I dropped the phone and ran. Out my office door, down the hall, down the steps.

My car was parked in my usual space. Right where I'd left it. Tree limbs bent in the wind and leaves slapped at a sky drained of color.

* * *

When I opened my eyes, I was in a hospital bed.

I lay in a calm room under cool sheets. A short, fat nurse stood beside me, but she didn't have a star tattoo or blue eyes. The eyes tucked back in her doughy face were as bright and green as apples.

"Well," she said, "you're back."

I took a deep breath and felt my septum throb.

When I groaned, she said, "After your jaw locked up they had to put the tube in through your nose. It may hurt for a while." She patted my arm. "You can get some more sleep if you want. Once you're feeling a little better some people are going to want to talk to you."

"Okay."

It was odd to hear my voice.

She put a hand on me as if to heal me with her love. "You're going to be okay," she ordered.

I didn't know what to say to that.

"I guess so," I said.

"You are going to be okay," she told me, even more firmly, like you would tell a kid he was going to eat his veggies. "It's none of my business, but not everyone gets a second chance. That many pills ..." She caught herself and issued a terse smile. "All I'm saying is, life is too precious to throw away."

When she left, I lay there in bed with what was left of my precious life.

And thought, *Goddamn it*.

The Nurse with the Black Star 2

I stared at the turquoise curtain pulled halfway around my bed. To my left was a Plexiglas partition. Blurred figures moved on the other side, and I heard the conversation between a couple of male nurses. I didn't pay them much attention, though. I just lay there and let my senses slowly come back to me.

My mind felt like a handful of photographs scattered on the floor. I knew I was Elliot Stilling. I knew I was in Little Rock, Arkansas. I knew that I had climbed through my ex-wife's bathroom window and washed down a bottle of pills with a bottle of whiskey. I remembered her bathroom floor, the cool tile, the pink bathmat. I remembered the soft descent into sleep.

Had Carrie come to see me yet? Was she waiting outside to see me? Had they told her I was awake? The thought of seeing her didn't frighten me. I don't know if it was a residual effect of the drugs, but I had trouble feeling anything at all. I wasn't angry or sad. I wasn't embarrassed. I wasn't suicidal. I was just a body on a bed. I leaned back into my pillows and closed my eyes, listening to my breathing, feeling the air in my lungs.

I was still listening and feeling when the young nurse with the black star appeared in the doorway to my room.

She wore teal scrubs, and though she was probably only in her late-twenties her cropped, punk-black hair was streaked with gray. Standing in the doorway holding a plastic pitcher, she announced bluntly, "Well, you're damn lucky to be here."

"So I've heard."

She strolled over to my bedside and picked up a plastic cup and filled it. Closer up, she looked rougher. Her blue eyes turned as hard as sapphires, and her mouth settled into a default skepticism. When she noticed me watching her, her spade-shaped jaw seemed to set, and lines formed around her mouth as she smiled.

Her name tag read: Felicia Vogan.

"Felicia …"

"That's my name," she said, handing me the water. "You need hydration. Can't have enough."

I drank the water in a gulp. "Thanks. May I have some more?" As she poured me another cup, I said, "You were in the emergency room."

She handed me the water. "Sure was."

"Are you the one who's supposed to be looking after me?"

"Nope. Just came to check on you."

"Is that the usual procedure?"

"No."

"So why'd you want to come see me?"

Amused she said, "You're pretty direct, aren't you?"

"I tried to kill myself yesterday. Ate a bottle of Dolophine. Now here I am. I don't have much left to be indirect about."

Those sapphires rarely blinked. "I suppose that's true."

"So why are you here if you don't have to be here?"

She leaned over the rail. "Well you made quite an impression, Reverend Stilling."

"Reverend?"

"That's what I hear," she explained. "The ER is required to document the contents of your wallet when you come in. They said there was a business card for Reverend Elliot Stilling."

"That's old."

"Oh."

"That was another … me. A year or so ago. I forget. Time's become kind of hard to keep track of. But I haven't been a preacher for a while."

"That makes sense."

"Why?"

"Well, we don't get many preachers trying to kill themselves."

"I suppose not."

She said, "I should probably go. Just wanted to say hello."

"That's it?"

"Should there be more?"

"No pep talk? The last nurse who was in here pretty much demanded that I acknowledge how wonderful life is."

We shared a smile for a moment before she said, "That's Tess. For Christmas one year she gave me a copy of *Chicken Soup for the Nurse's Soul*."

"Nice."

"I thought it was a cookbook."

"So you're not here to force a positive perspective on me?"

"I wouldn't have one to force on you even if I wanted to, Mr. Stilling."

"Call me Elliot."

"Elliot, I … you want to know the truth?"

"I do."

She held out her palm and pointed at the black star tattooed on her narrow wrist. "You grabbed me back in the ER."

"I know."

"You remember?"

"I remember seeing that star and grabbing your wrist. I remember seeing your face. You're the only thing I can remember."

"You grabbed me and looked right at me and right at the tattoo. Kind of freaked me out."

"I'm sorry."

"Don't be. I was startled, of course, but I was happy you were back. Well, you were back for a while …"

"I passed out after that."

"No." She shook her head. "You died."

"I …"

"For three minutes."

A wave of dizziness came over me, as if I'd wandered too close to the edge of a long fall. It was what I had wanted when I ate that bottle of pills, of course, but I still had to shut my eyes to stop my head from spinning.

"Scary," she said.

I opened my eyes. She had moved closer.

"Hey, are you okay?" she asked. "I didn't mean to … I can be a little indelicate."

"I'm fine," I said. "It's just not everyday someone tells you that you successfully killed yourself."

"No," she said. "I guess not."

Outside the door to my room, announcements barked over a loudspeaker, orderlies pushed carts, families asked questions, and the whole machine of the hospital whirled and clanged and spat.

Inside my room Felicia asked me, "How do you feel?"

"Alone," I said. "But less so since you walked in here."

Felicia Vogan took a moment to think about that. She sucked in her lips and then pushed them back out again before she said, "I'm glad, Elliot. I really am."

The doughy nurse walked in and said, "Hey, Felicia."

Felicia straightened up. "Hey, Tess."

Tess walked over to my bed and patted Felicia's back. "You checking on our boy?"

"Yep. Just wanted to tell him we're all pulling for him."

"Absolutely," Tess said. To me she said, "You feeling okay, sweetie? You need anything?"

"My clothes would be nice."

With an emphatic shake of her head, she told me, "Doctor Yaccoby wants you to stay in bed for just a little bit longer."

"Is that a fact?"

"Yep, and considering she saved your life yesterday, I'd think about taking her advice."

"You didn't lose my clothes, did you?"

Tess smiled. "No, baby. Your clothes are over there." She motioned vaguely to my right. "But for now you need to rest. You've been through a traumatic event, and your body needs to heal itself. You also need to talk to some people. Doctor Yaccoby will want to talk to you, as will a really nice specialist named Judy. We all just want to help you."

I mumbled something affirmative.

Satisfied, she turned to Felicia. "You on your way home, girl?"

"Yeah."

"Okay," Tess said. "I'll see you next week."

When she'd left, Felicia smiled at me. "I should go too," she said.

"Okay."

"It was nice meeting you, Elliot."

"It was the best part of my day," I said. "Of course, it's been a profoundly shitty day, but still ..."

With mock self-effacement, she said, "Nothing a girl likes to hear more than she was the best part of a day that started with being dead."

I laughed at that—and the sound of my laugh seemed like the faint echo of some forgotten time. It nearly made me cry.

She placed a warm hand on my shoulder. "Anything I can get you before I go?"

"Your phone number."

She withdrew her hand. "I don't think that's a good idea."

"I know," I said.

"I would get into a lot of trouble."

"I know. Can't blame a guy for trying."

She searched my face like she was trying to find something important there. "I just …"

"Really," I said. "I know. You don't have to explain why you'd turn down a digit request from a guy who killed himself last night."

She smiled. "Digit request?"

"I was one of those really cool preachers."

"Take care of yourself, Elliot."

"I'll try. You take care, too."

She leaned down and kissed my forehead. I hadn't smelled a woman's skin in almost two years. It made my mouth water.

"Isn't kissing the patients against some kind of hospital code?" I asked.

"I'm a really cool nurse."

After she left, I lay there a moment.

The room lightly hummed in climate controlled stillness. The humming started to squeeze my head. I felt the first burst of energy I'd had in months. I was damned if I was going to sit there and wait to be lectured by a doctor or some specialist. I'd be damned if I was going to wait until Carrie showed up.

I got out of bed. Getting my balance was a chore at first. The cold hospital floor was like an ice rink under my wobbly legs. I grabbed the end of the bed and just stood there for a while, letting my legs turn solid again. Once I was sure I wasn't going to fall over, I took a step. It was like trying to walk without any shins, and I damn near fell on my face. I waited, and then I took another step. It was a little better. I took another step and let go of the bed. My knees settled into it, and I pulled back the curtain. The room was empty. There were three other beds waiting for customers and a big green clothes cabinet against the far wall. Next to the cabinet, a large chart listed various types of choking hazards.

I walked toward the cabinet, still a little uncertain of my legs, but I could feel them again, and it felt good to be up.

I got to the cabinet and eased open its creaky door. Glancing over my shoulder, and feeling satisfied no one was back there, I opened it all the way and scooped out my clothes and shoes. I shut the door and hobbled back over to the nearest bed and pulled the curtain.

Once I investigated the clothes I realized the pants, socks and shoes were mine, but the shirt was not. It figured the ER people would have cut my shirt off in the operating room, but there were two shirts mixed in with my stuff. One was a white T-shirt three sizes too small for me. The other was a clean khaki work shirt with a name badge reading: Juan.

I opted for Juan's work shirt. I don't know if it was the drugs or not, but my fingers had a difficult time with the buttons on the shirt and a nearly impossible time with the button on the pants. But once I got warmed up, it was like walking. I got my shoes on.

"Let's get out of here," I said.

Good. Talking in the first person plural. That's normal, Elliot.

I cracked open the door and peered out. I didn't see Felicia or anyone else. I was about to step into the hall when I glanced over and saw a small phone book mixed in with some papers on a wooden table by the door. I picked it up and walked out.

In the hall, I kept my head mostly in the book, peering up enough to navigate down the hall. My gamble was that I could blend into the causal bustle in the hallway, but there wasn't really any bustle to be found.

Still, no one bothered me. At the end of the hall, I crept by the nurses' station while two nurses worked to extricate a cartridge from the busted printer below the desk. I headed for the exit. When I was almost there a young couple burst in—the boy moaning and clutching a bloody hand, the girl being a little too loud about it—and I tucked the phone book under my arm and strolled right out the door and into the dripping afternoon heat.

Exodus 3

My face hurt. Or, to be more precise, the inside of my face hurt. Breathing felt like a crime I was committing against my head, so I tried inhaling slowly, gently. I walked, taut and awkward, past patients and families in the unloading area, waiting to hear someone yell my name and tell me to get back to bed. But no one did.

I hadn't recognized the hospital from the inside, but once I'd waded into the humidity outside and had my bearings I realized I was at the UAMS hospital in Little Rock. It sat at the top of a long drive, its buildings and auxiliaries scattered over a couple of hills. I'd have to clomp down the hill to busy West Markham Street, and I wasn't quite up for that yet. In fact, after escaping the hospital, I wasn't quite up for anything. I ditched the phone book, walked over to a bench and plopped down next to a couple of sweating, middle-aged guys in jeans, work shirts, and boots. It had just rained and the bench was wet, but neither of them seemed to notice.

One guy rubbed his enormous gut thoughtfully. He wore wide blue suspenders to hold up his jeans, and when he was done rubbing his gut, he moved his hand up to one of the straps on his suspenders and tugged at it.

His friend, a craggy-faced man with thick sideburns, was slouched over, his elbows on his knees. He smoked a cigarette and stared at the parking lot like it was a mystery.

"All we can do is wait," the fat guy said.

The smoker rubbed his eyes with his thumb, and smoke wafted into his hair. "It's harder for me. I know she's your sister, but …" He stopped and took a drag off his cigarette.

"All we can do is wait," the fat guy said again. "That's all we can do."

The smoker wore a wedding ring. He fondled it with his thumb. "I reckon that's true."

I closed my eyes and rubbed my sinuses.

A truck passed us going a little too fast for the hospital parking lot. The smoker finished his cigarette and said again, "I reckon that's true," and flipped the burning filter into the truck's cloud of exhaust. With a deep breath, he stood up. "Well, let's do this."

"You ready?" the fat guy asked.

"No," the smoker grunted, and he turned and started for the hospital. The fat guy hoisted himself off the bench and started after his brother-in-law.

I just sat there feeling the sun on my face. Though the air sweltered, I still felt cold. Sweat rolled down my clammy face.

Off to my right, the front doors of the hospital slid open and Felicia walked out. Sunlight glinted off her hair, and she lifted her hand to her eyes. I watched her dig a pack of cigarettes out of a large handbag, stick a cigarette in her mouth, and cup her hand over a lighter. She had trouble getting it to work.

She was still trying to light her cigarette when a shiny new silver Zephyr rolled up to the curb about twenty feet away from me. The passenger side door opened and suddenly there was Carrie.

She didn't see me. She put one foot out the door and leaned back to gather her purse.

I turned on my hip, away from her. I couldn't face her.

To someone in the car she asked, "Do you want me to wait for you?"

"If you want to," a man said. His voice was deep.

Carrie said, "Okay," and closed the door.

"Do you, Elliot, take this woman to have and to hold, in sickness and in health, as long as you both shall live?"

A ringlet of hay-colored hair against her forehead. Her smile as I say "I do."

Carrie's new friend drove off. The bumper sticker on his car had a picture of Robert E. Lee and the words: AMERICA NEEDS A HERO.

Carrie walked up to the sliding doors but stopped and waited, pulling out her cell phone to text. The man with her must have nabbed a great parking spot because he made it to the doors not long after she did. He was a little older, maybe ten or fifteen years her senior, with salt-and-pepper hair and a small paunch. She put away her phone and took his hand. I'd never seen her with another man. They went in together. Supportive. Nice.

I stood up and walked across the parking lot. Felicia was gone. I'd missed my chance to catch her. At the edge of the parking lot, with no one to talk to, I just kept moving.

* * *

As I drifted up West Markham, past a dry cleaners and a Domino's Pizza, I thought about Carrie and her new friend moseying into my hospital room. Who was he? Where had they met? Some kind of support group? Online dating? At church?

Was he helping her get over what I had done to her?

No!

I would not think of it. I would consign that to the past, to the life I ended yesterday.

I thought about him instead. Would he go into the hospital room with her? Probably not. Maybe he'd kiss her worried brow and wait outside. *I'll be here if you need me,* he'd say. He'd stand there, arms folded, nodding at the orderlies, maybe checking out the asses of the nursing staff. After a few minutes Carrie would walk out, dazed, *He's gone. They lost him. Can you believe it?* Then he would put his arms around her and whisper, *Shh, it's okay,* as she cried, but he'd be thinking to himself, *This ex-husband is a real piece of work.*

At the intersection at the bottom of the road, I walked to the street corner, leaned on a wet trashcan at the edge of a Walgreens parking lot and waited for the light to change. As I waited, Felicia walked out of the store with a new cigarette lighter.

I thought about calling to her, but she saw me first.

"Elliot."

She seemed surprisingly unsurprised, as if we were old friends who'd bumped into each other.

"Hi," I said. I walked over to her.

"What are you doing?"

"Walking."

"You should be in bed."

"Yeah."

"Did you … follow me?"

"Yes." What the hell. There was no point in lying.

"What was your plan exactly?"

"Do I look like a man with a plan?"

She laughed. "No, Elliot, you don't." She smiled now at her own craziness. Resigned to it, she said, "Well, can I give you a lift somewhere?"

"Should you really do that?"

"Hell no, I shouldn't, but I'm a congenital pushover for sad sacks and deadbeats."

"Is that what I am?"

"If you're not, then no one is."

I gestured down the road. "I don't … I don't actually have anywhere to go. I wouldn't know where to ask you to take me."

She twirled her keys around her finger. "Do you want to get a drink?"

I almost laughed at that. "That what I need five minutes after walking out of a hospital? Alcohol?"

"No. You need plenty of rest and fluids. Preferably lots of water. But what I *asked* you was if you *wanted* alcohol."

"Yes."

"Then get in."

I walked over to her car and got inside.

We pulled out of the parking lot and when the light changed, she crossed West Markham. She went uphill into the neighborhoods, but neither of us said anything for a while. Felicia kept the windows down, either to smoke or because the AC didn't work. Either way the summer humidity hung on everything: me, her, the sagging trees, the damp lawns and sidewalks. The car was an older Ford Escort cluttered with trash and smelling of cigarettes and fast food. She wouldn't be thin for too much longer if this was the way she lived.

Then it occurred to me that I needed money for booze. I reached for my pocket. My wallet wasn't there. Hell of a day.

We passed some nice old houses—not mansions by any means, but spacious enough and old enough to be classy, with small verandas and tiny patches of green grass giving off the faint impression of property. On a couple of those verandas people sat fanning themselves in the late afternoon heat, sipping store-bought lemonade and pretending they were real Southerners. At the end of the day, I felt certain they would just go back inside and turn on the TV and crank up the AC like everybody else.

"I live just up the road a bit," she said. "You don't mind if we stop so I can change out of my work clothes, do you?"

"No. That's fine. You're the one driving."

She lit up a cigarette while using her elbows to steer the car.

"This is a nice neighborhood," I said.

"Yeah, it is. I live in my dad's old house." She took a drag and flicked ashes out the window. "It's all he left me with."

"He died?"

"Yeah."

"I'm sorry to hear that."

She shrugged. As she steered the car, smoke curled off her cigarette and dissipated against the windshield. "He couldn't afford the house. He couldn't afford half the crap he ever bought. I don't want to speak ill of him, you know. I loved him, but he had money problems and then …"

"He died."

She stopped at a crosswalk to let an elderly couple walk by.

"He killed himself, actually."

"Oh, God."

I felt a sudden rush of guilt.

"I'm so sorry," I told her, more in the way of an apology than a condolence.

"No, I'm sorry," she said.

"For what?"

"Well, I don't know how sensitive you are about, uh …"

"The whole suicide thing?"

She grinned. "Yeah. I guess."

"I admire bluntness."

"Good. Me too. I guess that's why we hit it off back at the hospital." She flicked ashes that sucked back through the window and scattered over the trash in the backseat. "I don't really tiptoe around things. I've always been like that, and I guess nursing's only made me more that way. Hell, I guess life has made me more that way. I mean, after Dad killed himself, I got saddled with a heap of debts and an old house." She flicked more ashes. "Thanks, Dad."

Guilt pulled my face down. I examined my palms. "I really am so sorry to hear that, Felicia. That's an awful thing to have to go through."

"Yeah. It is. And I'm not just trying to make you feel bad. I hope you know that."

"I know."

"That's why I got the star." She held up her wrist as if I hadn't seen it before. "To remind me."

I stared out the window at the cars parked along the sun-dappled street. They all belonged to people. Those people all had lives. Those lives were going on in those houses. Just one neighborhood in a little corner of Little Rock, but at that moment it seemed like the vastness of all the world.

"You try selling your dad's house?" I asked. "To get out from under everything, maybe start over fresh?"

"Sure, for the last two years I've tried to sell it. It's a pretty house—you'll see it—but the housing market dropped out right about the time I started trying to unload it."

We slowed near the top of the hill. Felicia frowned at something ahead of us.

I saw only a tree lined street. Some cars parked along the side of road.

At the bottom of the hill below us, a garbage truck rumbled by. Somewhere in the trees a woodpecker hammered away. But Felicia kept looking at whatever she was looking at.

I was about to ask her if something was wrong when she said, "Shit."

"What is it?" I asked.

She didn't answer me, but I saw that she was staring at a dark blue Nissan Armada SUV parked on the side of the road at the end of a long rising driveway. "That son of a bitch," she said.

She threw the car in reverse, but as she did a police cruiser sped up the street. It whipped up to us and stopped just short of her bumper. Felicia grunted and slammed the car in park.

A cop jumped out and ran up to her. Crew cut and barrel-chested, he had arms like tree trunks. He thrust his head in her window and snapped, "Who the fuck is this guy, Felicia?"

The Twins   4

"Goddamn it, DB—" she started.

"C'mon," he said. "Let's go. Out of the car." He opened her door and jerked his cleft chin at me. "You too, asshole. Out of the car."

As she stepped out of the car, he took her elbow like she was a senile old woman who'd slipped away from the house.

"Get your fucking hands off me," she said, jerking her arm back.

I got out of the car, and the cop kept his eyes on me. He rested his thumb on the handle of his gun.

He jerked his chin at me. "Who the fuck are you?"

"Just another taxpayer."

"Don't smart off to me, dipshit. I asked you for your name."

I just stared at him.

He pointed at Felicia and demanded, "Who is this?"

"He's a guy I met at the hospital. What the fuck's your problem, DB? And why is the Armada parked outside my house?"

"I asked you who this guy is."

"I just told you. We met at the hospital. I was his nurse. And now we were going to get drinks. That's the whole story of me and this guy."

"Drinks at your house?"

"I was coming home to change, asshole. *Then* we were going to get drinks."

"Drinks with a patient. That a new service the hospital is providing?"

"I—"

"Shut up," he told her.

"He doesn't know anything about ... our stuff," Felicia said.

The cop had small, stupid eyes sunk deep into aggressive bone structure. He moved toward me with his right hand never more than an inch from his black handgun. His eyes leveled on me with simple-minded intensity. He was not the kind of man you want to meet under any circumstances, but especially not the kind of man you want to meet when he's wearing a badge.

"That true?" he asked.

I shrugged.

He asked, "How'd you like to go to jail today?"

"For what?"

He stepped toward me and leaned close enough to my face that I could smell the coffee on his breath. "You watch your tone with me, asshole."

"Yes, sir."

"You want to go to jail?"

"No, sir."

"Then beat it. If you really were about to hook up with Felicia here, word around town is you ain't missing much."

Felicia crossed her arms and stayed silent.

DB took a step back to let me move. "Beat it," he said.

When I didn't move, he said, "You got a problem?"

I didn't budge. I could've left, but I didn't want to. I've always been a physical coward, and I've always been afraid of cops. But I did not move. It was as if I'd been asked a much larger question. For a spilt second it seemed as if I might be able to walk away from whatever was going on between them, but just as quickly I knew that I couldn't just walk off. Something bad was happening here, and even if I ran away as fast as I could I knew I wouldn't be able to go far enough or fast enough to shake the feeling that I'd made a horrible choice.

I said, "I guess I can't just leave her like this."

DB laughed and turned to Felicia. "What, this dude is like your bodyguard?"

She said, "He's my friend, DB. My new friend. That good enough for you?"

DB turned back to me and his demeanor thawed a bit. "Look, pal. I ain't her boyfriend. Okay? We're just business acquaintances who need to talk, that's all. Why don't you take a hike? Go get yourself another skank."

I gestured at his badge number and said, "If I leave, I just might have to report this incident, Officer 16781."

DB smiled at me contemptuously. "Well, that was a stupid thing to say."

* * *

He loaded me into the backseat of his patrol car, without handcuffs or any sense that I was being arrested but also without any sense that I had a say in the matter, and we followed Felicia up the long driveway to her house. We didn't speak to each other, and I watched the back of Felicia's head.

The long narrow drive hedged on one side by long row of Chokeberry bushes and on the other side by a tall wooden fence. At the top of the drive, Felicia parked at the end of the wide veranda of a white, two-story house. DB pulled up behind her.

"Get out," he said.

We walked through the front yard toward the side of the house where Felicia had parked. Sunlight shimmered on the windows, and raindrops beaded the awnings like sweat. The shades were all lifted in the front rooms, and through floor-length windows I saw a dining room with polished hardwood floors, a long table with a full set of chairs, and an antique chandelier hanging from a steepled ceiling. Beyond the dining room, an open door led into a sitting room filled with bookshelves. At the other end of the dining room, through another open door, I saw the end of a kitchen island.

"Hey," DB snapped at me, "let's go."

He steered me around to the back of the house. A few paces ahead of us Felicia opened the screen door and stepped inside.

As we rounded a dying rose bush hugging the edge of the house, DB followed me so closely I could hear his breathing. He gestured to the narrow back steps leading into the kitchen. When I got to the door he reached in front of me and blocked my entry. Though he was shorter than I'd first noticed, he seemed composed purely of muscle and bone.

He pushed his face up to mine like fierce dog. "I don't know what the fuck you think you're doing, but you just dropped into a whole sewer full of shit."

I tilted away from him. "Okay," I said.

He opened the door and allowed me to go in first.

It was an old house. The screen door groaned, and the plate glass window in the heavy kitchen door rattled as DB closed it behind us. The kitchen had high ceilings, a green-tiled backsplash, and a long island. Over a sink filled with dirty dishes hung a suncatcher in the shape of a cross. DB nodded toward the book-lined den.

"What the hell?" Felicia exclaimed.

Standing in the den, his fists lifted to his hips, was another man. It took me a moment to accept what I was seeing: he was another version of DB. He wasn't wearing a cop's uniform, but he was clearly DB's twin brother, right down to his cleft chin and the beady meanness in his close-set eyes. The only difference seemed to be the cochlear implants over his ears.

The twin signed something to his brother.

"Found him with her," DB said.

Felicia turned to DB and demanded, "What the hell is Tom doing in my house?"

"We're just a little concerned about you is all," DB explained.

The twin resembled a bank teller who'd spent the night sleeping in a gutter. He wore a rumpled dress shirt with a loosened green tie and grimy slacks. He cocked his head at his brother and glanced down at Felicia and signed something. Without knowing sign language, I was still pretty sure he'd said, *What the fuck? Why'd you bring him here?*

"I saw them together," DB said. "He was with her in the car."

"Wait a second," Felicia said. "Were you following me? Did you tail me home from work?"

"It's an important day," he said by way of an explanation. "Plus, we don't really trust you."

"You two don't have to trust me," she said. "Stan trusts me. That's enough."

"Maybe Stan trusts you. But that don't matter to me and Tom if our asses are on the line."

Quiet Tom operated like his brother's shadow. Silent but wholly in synch, he seemed tuned to DB's every move. I got the distinct impression that if DB ordered Tom to kill me, he would do it without hesitating.

"So, you see it as your job to tail me home from work and interrogate me because you see me with some guy?"

"Today's a big day like I said. Awful damn peculiar of you to take time out to make a new boyfriend."

Felicia dropped onto an antique chair. She seemed perfectly at home in the house, but at the same time, the place seemed too old for her. It felt like the home of elderly people, not a single woman under thirty.

She ran her hand through her hair and regarded me for an instant. Silent thoughts flickered dimly in her blue eyes. She chewed her lip.

Finally she asked DB, "Where's Stan?"

"He's around."

"Get him over here."

"I'll text him."

"Do that. I want to discuss this new development." She stood up and told me, "Elliot, you come with me."

"Where you two going?" DB asked.

"To my bedroom," she snapped. "For some privacy from you two assholes. Get Stan over here so we can all have a talk. You two let yourselves into my house, so please, *please*, make yourselves at home."

With that she turned and left the room. I sat there a moment, unsure of what to do. The twins made eye contact and started signing to each other.

"Excuse me," I said and stood up and followed Felicia.

Felicia's Room 5

I followed her through a dining room with polished hardwood floors and a long dining table, past a little white-tiled half-bath, and into a master bedroom. A four-post bed stood against pale blue walls that climbed nine feet to a vaulted ceiling. An enormous gray and navy rug covered most of the floor. A door opened into a white-tiled master bath with a sliding glass door. The place was neat, lovely, and oddly quaint for a young woman.

Felicia said, "You can sit down on the bed if you want."

I sat down and watched as she opened the double doors on a deep closet of clothes.

Without turning around, she said, "I guess I owe you an explanation."

"I'm not sure you owe me anything," I said "but I'd appreciate it."

She pulled out a pair of jeans and black tank top. As she carried them over to a dresser she said, "The thing of it is, I don't know what I should tell you." She opened a drawer and pulled out a wine-colored underwear set. "Should I tell you everything or nothing? It's not too late for you to go, but if you do want to go time is running out." She carried her clothes to the door of the master bath. "On the other hand, it's not too early for you to decide to stay, either. It should be obvious, just based on how intense these assholes are, that this deal is real. You know I need the money. Maybe you do, too. I don't know. But there is money to be made if you want to make it."

She went into the bathroom and closed the door. I heard water run in the shower.

I leaned down and put my face in her pillows and inhaled the promise of her skin and hair. My eyes watered. I pressed against her pillow until the water shut off in the bathroom. Then I sat up.

After a few minutes, she came out freshly showered and dressed, sat on the bed and tucked one leg under the other. Her wet hair dripped down onto skin that smelled clean and warm and moist. For a moment, she examined my face like a jeweler searching for flaws.

"Well?" she said. "What do you think of what I said?"

"Will they let me stay?"

"If I say you're with me, and if you don't take any of their cut of the money, then yes."

"What about this Stan guy? Is he the boss?"

"Pretty much. He's the one everyone is afraid of, anyway, which is the same thing."

I nodded. "I want to stay."

"What kind of cut do you need?"

"I don't give a shit about money."

"You independently wealthy?"

"I don't have a dime to my name."

"Then why don't you care about money?"

"I just don't."

She frowned as if I'd tried to convince her that down was up. "So, why would you stay?"

"Because there's nothing else for me. I have no life outside of this house, nowhere else to go. I killed myself yesterday, Felicia. I ended my life. And then, somehow, I woke up this morning in a new life. This one here with you. So I don't know what else to do. Either I live this life or I kill myself again."

Felicia ran both of her hands through her hair and laced her fingers together behind her head. "Jesus." She pursed her lips. "Okay."

"So tell me. Who are these people? What are they doing?"

She dropped her hands in her lap. "God, where to start?"

"Start at the beginning. Who's Stan?"

"He's … a criminal's criminal, I guess you'd say. He's got his hand in a lot of things. Burglary. Drugs. Hijacking."

"How'd you get involved with him?"

"I was dating a guy. Fuller. Fuller works with Stan occasionally. I was really into drugs at that point, drugs and bad boys. I was smoking dusted weed, popping pills, hooking up with shady guys. Sometimes I'd steal pills and syringes for Fuller. Then one night he introduced me to Stan. And, at first, Stan scared me because he was the only guy Fuller seemed to be afraid of. Plus, he's just weird. He always seemed to be off in his own head. He'd start talking about random stuff all of the sudden. I just didn't get him.

"Then Fuller and I broke up, and I stopped doing drugs. Went into recovery. Stopped hanging out with all of those guys. I was doing okay for a while. Exercising, eating right, reading. And then one night, Stan showed up here with a knife wound. Somebody had stabbed him over … something. I don't know what it was, but they stuck a six-inch blade through his navel. I helped him. After that, we started hanging out, even though I wasn't doing drugs anymore."

"Nice guy to hang out with, a drug dealer you stitch up after a knife fight."

Felicia said, "I'm being reprimanded by a suicide?"

"Sorry. Must be the residual preacher in me. I'm just saying this Stan guy seems like the wrong type to hang around with."

"I know," she said. "But that was why, of course. I like bad boys. Or usually I do. Stan's not bad in the usual way, though. He's not being a badass to impress girls. He's bad in a weird, fucked up way."

"What about the twins?"

She waved them away. "DB's a little man with a badge. Tom's a little man without a badge. Together they're about as dangerous as a junior high food fight."

"They seem dangerous to me."

"I can handle them. Stan's the wild card. When this deal goes down, he's the one to watch."

"And just what is the deal?"

She stood up and walked to other side of the room and listened at the door. Content with whatever she heard or thought she heard, she walked back to the bed. She didn't sit down, though. She stood over me and stared at me with those sharp blue eyes and said, "If I tell you what's going down, it means you're in on it. You're locked in."

"I know."

She nodded.

"The hospital gets in daily shipments of supplies. Scrubs, catheters, needles. Whatever. It all goes through the shipping and receiving dock at the distribution center and gets processed by the materials management office. All except for the pharmaceuticals. For insurance reasons, all the drugs go up a short alley on the back of Ward Tower and go straight to the pharmacy where they're held in a bulk storage vault. The trucks back in, unload onto a service elevator, and go straight up to the vault. The vault is covered by surveillance cameras, and you have to have a bar-coded ID badge to get in. Past 7 p.m., you can't get into the vault at all. Sets off an alarm at the hospital central control.

"But tonight's different. In the last few months, you might have heard about this big drug company price-fixing scandal on the news?"

"I haven't exactly been keeping up with the news."

"No. Well, last year the government sued a bunch of pharmaceutical companies for overcharging drugs covered by Medicaid. The government won the lawsuit, and one of companies that lost was this generic retailer, Activity Plus. They got busted overcharging medical providers, including UAMS, for prescription meds. The lawsuit bankrupted Activity Plus and they're going out of business. Part of the settlement is that they're unloading their stock at a discount to all of the hospitals they overcharged."

"Which, I take it, brings us to tonight."

"Exactly. Tonight they're bringing in a big bulk shipment of Oxycodone." She stopped. "You know what that is?"

"Like Oxycontin."

"One and the same. The truck should be carrying sixteen pallets of Oxy. That's somewhere in the neighborhood of eighty thousand 80mg Oxycodones."

"Shit."

"Yes, shit. Shit, exactly."

"Is Stan gonna keep them?"

"No, he's not looking to get into the drug lord business. That's too long term. He's a thief. He just wants to grab the shipment and turn around and sell it. He's got a buyer set up."

"How much is the haul from a shipment that large?"

"A cool two million."

"My God."

She nodded and spread her palms out. "Take the truck before it unloads. Take the loot to the buyer. Get the cash."

"Who's the buyer?"

"Fuller."

"Your ex-boyfriend."

"Yes."

I sat back against her pillows. "That's a hell of a deal."

"It is."

"A hell of a deal. I guess my only question is, why are you telling me about it?"

She sat down on the bed next to me. "Because back there when DB told you to get lost, you didn't." Her leg touched mine. "These guys needed me for the information about the hospital and the shipment. They don't really need me now. And while they don't have any reason to fuck me over now that the deal's going down, guys like this don't always need a reason. The money is reason enough."

"You want someone watching your back."

"Yes."

"I've never considered myself a physically imposing man. Or a brave man."

"But you didn't run. You didn't give DB your name. Your impulse was to stay put and stay quiet. You had my back for no reason at all. But now you do have a reason. I can give you a piece of my cut of the money."

"I told you, Felicia, I don't care about money. I never did, and I care less about it right now than I ever have. I just want to be ... to stay close by you. If you want me here, then I want to stay."

Those hard eyes seemed to soften. "You really don't have anywhere else to go, do you?"

"No."

"What happened to you?"

Leaning back further into her pillows, I closed my eyes.

I dropped the phone and ran. Out my office door, down the hall, down the steps.

My car was parked in my usual space. Right where I'd left it. Tree limbs bent in the wind and leaves slapped at a sky drained of color.

I opened my eyes. She reached over and took my hand.

"Tell me," she said. "What happened?"

I pulled my hand back. "No."

"I don't—"

"That's all I want from you," I said. "You don't have to sleep with me and you don't have to give me any money. Just don't ask me about my last life. Ever."

She drew back her hand and rubbed it as if it had gone numb.

"Okay," she said.

Stan the Man 6

A few minutes later, DB called from the dining room, "He's here."

Felicia stood up and slipped on some black thong sandals. She nodded and said, "Are you ready to meet Stan the Man?"

I followed her through the dining room to the open front door where DB and Quiet Tom stood waiting like disciples. Leaving me there, Felicia hurried past the twins and rushed down the steps to the tall man who was walking up the driveway.

Stan the Man had scarlet hair and an ax-shaped face hoisted high on a scrawny neck. As he led Felicia back up to the house, he hunched over her, a long arm clamped around her shoulders, his face close to her ear. As they moved from under a leafy canopy of shade into the sunlight, his slicked-back hair blazed a brilliant orange and his off-white suit shone like white fire. A fat knot of an Adam's apple jutted up and down in his neck when he said, "I never like to discuss bidness outside, darlin'."

Felicia said, "I just wanted a chance to explain—"

He clutched her elbow and guided her up the steps. "Aw, you can wait," he said. "Ain't heard the explanation yet couldn't be improved by air conditioning."

Stan let Felicia enter first. Then he walked in behind her, closed the front door, slipped his long hands into the pockets of his suit coat and stared at me.

"I hear we have a new bidness associate."

"Stan—" DB started.

Stan's right hand flashed out of his pocket, a slender finger lifted. "Wait," he said. He pointed at me. "How about you take it, brother."

Except for rutted acne scars on his cheeks, Stan's face was smooth and pale. It was difficult to tell how old he was, and in some ways, with his off-white suit and lanky frame, he had the air of a geeky boy preacher. Then his thin lips disappeared into his serpentine mouth as he began to smile at me, and something changed. With his scarlet hair smoothed back against his scalp and his money-green eyes picking me apart, he suddenly looked more like Satan's nasty kid brother.

He said, "You do talk don't you, boy? We already got our-selves a mute."

"I talk."

"Then do so."

Before I could reply, DB jerked his thumb at Felicia. "He's with her. She wants to bring him in on the deal."

"I didn't ask you nothing," Stan told DB, "so be quiet and let the man speak." His reedy voice had an oddly fickle quality, thin one moment and thick as cream the next.

DB said petulantly, "I was just going to say Felicia wants to bring him in."

Quiet Tom signed something to his brother.

"Shut up," DB answered him. "I'm the goddamn cop here."

"Boys, boys," Stan chided. There was some inner calculus going on. Stan read people, and he had begun to read me. I'm not sure what he saw on my life-battered face, but I think he could tell I was the only one in the room who wasn't afraid of him yet.

Felicia filled the small silence with, "This is Elliot, and he—"

"I didn't ask you shit, Felicia," Stan snapped.

Then he pointed at the kitchen and told me, "Why don't we go in here and have us a little powwow? Just the two of us. That way we can talk without all this butting in."

I glanced at Felicia. She walked over to the dining room table and sat down and stared at her hands. I don't know what I wanted from her just then, but she gave me nothing.

Stan watched me watch her, and he gestured toward the kitchen.

"Sure," I said.

He strolled into the kitchen, and I followed him. He stopped at the sink, his back to me, and turned on the water.

"I take it you're sweet on Felicia," he said.

It seemed too complicated to explain, so I just said, "I guess."

"What's your name? Not Juan."

I touched the name tag on my shirt and realized he was watching my reflection in the window. I leaned against the wall and let him watch.

"Elliot Stilling," I said.

"Elliot Stilling. That name sounds familiar. You somebody I heard of?"

"I'm nobody."

"Nobody's nobody."

"Most people are nobody."

Stan shut off the water and turned around. His white suit coat was unbuttoned. He wore an olive shirt with a cardinal tie, and everything appeared freshly cleaned and pressed. He dried his hands on a dish towel.

"Well, I suppose that's true, Elliot." He tossed the towel on the sink and slid his hands into his pockets. "How do you know Felicia?"

"From the hospital."

"Ah. Yes. Course. Felicia makes lots of friends that way."

"I suppose."

"You fucking her?"

"Pardon?"

He smiled. "I love a feller with manners. I asked if you was fornicating with Felicia."

"No," I said. "I'm not."

"Why not?"

"What?"

His smooth face reddened, but he kept smiling. "Now, I hate repeating myself, Elliot. For you and me to get along you're gonna need to grab holt of that pretty quick. I absolutely motherfucking hate to repeat myself."

"I'm sorry. Your question threw me off a little."

"Felicia ain't exactly famous for her discriminating taste in sexual partners," Stan explained. "And she don't have platonic relationships with the men folks. So when you say you ain't fucking her, it sorta smells like bullshit to me."

"We just met."

"Just when?"

"Today."

That seemed to genuinely surprise him, but he just sucked on his bottom lip. "Hmm." He thought about it for a moment. When he'd thought about it enough, he asked, "You in love with her?"

"I told you, we just met."

Stan raised his eyebrows. "Well, that ain't too soon to be in love if it was love at first sight." He squinted. "Was it love at first sight?"

"Not exactly."

"That's good."

"Why is it good?"

"Because men fuck Felicia. They don't fall in love with her."

"See," I said, "when you say that, it makes me want to save her."

Stan shook his head sadly. "If that's true, boy, you're pouring yourself a long tall drink of misery."

"Maybe, but that doesn't mean I have to be a problem for you."

"You're already a problem for me."

"Not too much of one, though."

"That's the question, isn't it? How big a pain in my ass are you going to be?"

"You think I'm here for the money?"

"Ain't you?"

"No. I'm here for the girl."

"Ah, but the girl is here for the money."

I didn't know what to say to that.

"You see the problem," Stan said.

"I suppose."

"What do you know about the money?"

"Just about nothing."

"You tell me what you know, and I'll judge how close it is to nothing."

I told him what she'd told me about the robbery. I wasn't sure if I should, but Felicia had not indicated in any way that I should play dumb about what was going on, so I told him all I knew.

When I was finished, Stan said, "It's a heap of cash."

"Yes, it is."

"I wonder how come she told you about it."

I shrugged. "Maybe she likes me." When he smirked at that, I said, "I know that might be hard for you to believe, but it is the truth."

"The truth," Stan mused. "Well now, maybe it is, and maybe it ain't. But I like things that make sense."

"And you don't think Felicia having feelings for me makes sense."

"Well," Stan answered, "Felicia's feelings don't always come together to form a unified whole, if you catch my meaning. There are two or three different people running around in that girl's head."

I let that go, and Stan just stared at me for a moment— thinking and figuring and weighing the possibilities. I knew one of those possibilities probably involved blowing my brains out in the bathtub. But Stan wasn't stupid like DB and Quiet Tom. He thought about it for a while. Finally he said,

"Let's go talk to your blushing beauty. We'll see what she says." He pushed himself off the counter and nodded toward the dining room.

Neither Felicia nor the brothers had moved.

Stan stood beside me. He asked Felicia, "What's the deal with this guy?"

Felicia said, "I met him at the hospital. We hit it off."

"You hit it off. That's nice. But why is he here?"

She regarded me with genuine wonder. "I don't know. DB told him to get lost, but he wouldn't. He wanted to stay with me."

Stan shook his head. "No, no. I mean, *why* is he here? Why did you bring him in on this thing in the first place?"

Felicia pointed at DB. "I didn't. This dumb fucking cop here was tailing me, watching me—"

"I don't trust you," DB said.

"You think I trust you?"

She turned back to Stan. "Elliot and I were going to get drinks. That's all. But DB was following me and pulled us over on the street and practically dragged us out of the car. He was the one who tipped Elliot to the fact that there was something going down."

"You picked a strange time to get drinks with a stranger you just met at the hospital," Stan said. "On the day we're going to pull a two million dollar job."

Felicia ran her fingers through her damp hair. "I was taking him for drinks." Avoiding my eyes, she said, "And, yes, I was going to ask him, eventually, if he might be interested in the job."

"Without consulting me about it?" Stan asked.

"You said the job could use another guy."

"I said the job could use another guy. I didn't tell you to go recruiting for help at the fucking hospital. For all you know, I could have already lined up another guy."

"But you didn't, did you?"

"No."

"Well, now you have one."

Stan stood with his hands in the pockets of his slacks, shifting his weight back and forth from one foot to the other. He cocked his head and regarded first Felicia, then me.

He took a hand from his pocket and scratched his pointed chin. Finally he said, "Here's the deal, Elliot. Since Felicia brought you in on this thing, she's the one who'll have to take care of you. You want a cut of the cash, she's the one you talk to. Understand?"

"Yes."

DB stepped toward Stan. "You sure about that? We don't know this guy."

"She vouches for him," Stan said jerking his thumb in Felicia's general direction.

"You trust her?"

Stan admired the white linen of his jacket. "We're trusting her with the details of the job, ain't we? She's the one set this deal up in the first place, ain't she?"

"Yes," DB admitted.

"Well then, we can let her bring in a guy if she wants. We could use an extra hand on this deal, and he's not going to touch the cut. You got any objections?"

DB murmured, "I guess not," but he threw me a look as hard as a punch. I did not foresee a friendship forming.

Surveying all of us, though, Stan seemed pleased. It wasn't possible to tell how he was reading the situation, or what benefit he saw in having me around, but his face curled into a smile as he said, "That's settled then. Elliot is with us."

The Truck Job 7

Over the next hour or so, we sat in Felicia's sitting room and discussed details of the plan. Stan explained everything in his disconcertingly amiable way while Felicia listened quietly and the twins synchronized their twitches. I kept my mouth shut. Then, as the last dying rays of sunlight filled the room with a golden glow, Stan stood up and said, "Let's go for a ride."

"Ride?" DB said. "Where?"

"No, you boys stay here," he said. "I'm taking Felicia and Elliot here on a little field trip. Scope out the job and make sure Elliot is clear on the details."

Quiet Tom waited for his brother's response. DB held his tongue.

To break the silence I said, "Okay."

Stan smiled. "Nothing I like better than agreeable bidness associates."

Felicia's hair had dried and now jutted out at all angles like little punk-black thorns. She rubbed her bare arms and said, "I'm going to throw on something with sleeves."

Stan watched her get up and walk to her bedroom. "Get your keys," he called after her.

"Okay," she called back.

I stood up.

DB asked, "How long will you be?"

Stan's face stayed turned toward Felicia's room. "Few minutes," he said. "No more."

Felicia came back in. She wore a loose blue button-up with rolled up sleeves over her black tank top.

I followed her as Stan led us outside. The burning hell that is August in Arkansas had reached its peak hours before. As the exhausted day limped off into night, heat still clung to the air as a bad reminder of the brutal sun. I started sweating immediately.

Stan pointed at her car. "Felicia," he said, "you can drive. Elliot, you ride shotgun."

I walked to the passenger door. Felicia went to the driver's side and unlocked the car with a button on her keychain, but as she did Stan swooped in behind her and pinned her to her car.

"The fuck—" she grunted, dropping her keys.

In my moment of hesitation Stan said, "Elliot, stay put."

He pulled some kind of undersized revolver from the small of Felicia's back.

Keeping her pressed against the door with his body, he half-whispered into her ear, "What's this?"

"What's it look like?"

"It looks like you went to your room and got a gun and didn't tell me about it."

She grunted, "I gotta tell you every move I make? You tell me every move you make?"

"Why the gun?"

"Why not?"

He pressed even closer to her, so that his bony face mashed against her cheek when he spoke, "Where'd you get the gun?"

"It belonged to my dad."

Stan's eyes lifted to take me in.

"How you doing over there, Elliot?"

"She told you where it came from," I said. "She the only one here with a gun?"

He smiled. "She's the only one hiding one."

"I wasn't hiding it," she protested.

"Of course, you were. Why lie about it?"

"What do you want me to say?"

"I want you to say that you went and got the piece because you're afraid of me. You didn't know what I was going to do to you and Elliot, so you went and dug out your daddy's old .22 and stuck it in the back of your pants like they do in the movies."

"All that's true," she said.

"I know it is, darlin', but why do I got to be the one to say it?"

He stepped back and Felicia took a breath and slowly turned around to face him. He held out her gun.

She took it.

"Be careful with that," he said. "Guns don't kill people. People do."

He opened the back door and got inside.

* * *

Stan directed Felicia to show us the layout of the job.

She drove down Cedar Street and turned into the UAMS campus. We all stayed silent, though I didn't get the feeling that Stan was nervous. He seemed to just be sitting in the back, quietly taking in the sights. Felicia navigated through the complex of buildings and turned onto Elm Street.

"Slow down," Stan said.

As we passed by the Rockefeller Cancer Institute, Stan said, "Right here past the patient loading area, you see that little alley at the end of the building?"

"Yes," I said.

"That's it. Truck'll pull in there, do a series of turns inside the lot, and back up to the dock. We hide down the alley behind the cancer building, wait for the driver to pass us and make his turns and back up to the dock, and then we take him. But we don't grab him until he's completed his turns. We want a straight shot out of here."

"Seems like a good plan."

Felicia drove up Elm and turned onto another street.

Stan said, "Go over it for me one time if you would, Elliot."

"Felicia is the lookout at the entrance to Elm Street. She's in her car, keeping an eye out for the hospital police force and tipping us off when the truck arrives. DB is at the exit, monitoring the cops and what they know and when they know it, and providing interference for us if we need it. Quiet Tom drives us and drops us off in the parking lot of the Cancer Institute and sticks around as a getaway driver in case something goes wrong. When he drops us off, we hoof it over the alley, wait for the truck to show up and get into position, and then we rush it. You do all the talking. I hood and handcuff the driver. You drive. We meet at the rendezvous point."

I turned around. Stan smiled.

"We'll make a hijacker out of you yet, Elliot." He leaned back in his seat. "Felicia, we're done. Let's head back."

Night had settled, but no stars had come out. Above the illumination of the hospital lights, the sky hung low and black. I closed my eyes and listened to the tires on the pavement. My past life felt so distant at that point it seemed to have happened to someone else entirely.

That warm, numbing feeling didn't last long, though, because from the backseat, Stan said, "Tell me more about yourself, Elliot."

"What do you mean?"

Felicia glanced at me. She didn't have to say anything. We both knew Stan wasn't making idle conversation. Stan had probably never made idle conversation in his life.

"What do you do for a living?"

"I'm between things."

"What was the last thing?"

"I worked at a tobacco store."

"Which one?"

"Smokey's. In North Little Rock."

As casually as a smoker wipes an ash off his sleeve, I realized that I had not actually tendered my resignation at Smokey's Cigarette Emporium. I'd been at work there just a few days before. So much for that.

Stan said, "You seem overly educated to be peddling cigarettes for minimum wage."

I shrugged.

"What'd you do before that?" he asked.

We paused at a stop sign.

"I was a preacher," I said.

After a car passed through the intersection, Felicia drove us back up the hill she and I had taken just a few hours before.

Stan said, "A preacher."

"Yeah."

"What manner of preacher? What denomination?"

"Free-Will Baptist."

"I'll be doggone. You were out saving souls."

I looked over my shoulder at him. As we passed beneath street lights, he flickered in and out of darkness.

"I guess so," I said.

"And now you're here with me." He smiled and leaned back in his seat and closed his eyes. "That's beautiful."

* * *

When the time came, everyone seemed nervous, even Stan, though he didn't show it like everyone else. I sat on the sofa in the sitting room, tapping my foot incessantly. DB babbled about the details of the job to anyone who would listen while Quiet Tom nodded excessively at everything he said. Felicia paced the dining room, rubbing her hands together, expressing wonderment every few minutes about how moist her palms were. "I never sweat in the ER," she said no less than three times.

Stan stood at the window, staring outside. There was nothing for him to watch out there except the stillness of Felicia's driveway, but he stared at it anyway. The thing that marked him as nervous was his silence. He hadn't spoken a word—hadn't communicated with anyone in fact, since we'd returned to the house.

When the time came, he just said, "Let's go."

My own feeling of nervous expectation reminded me, oddly enough, of Sunday mornings. Getting dressed, making sure I had my bible and notes, preparing to be my public self. As I stood up to follow Stan, I took a deep breath—the first breath, it struck me, of Elliot Stilling, Professional Criminal.

DB left first. He went out to his patrol car without a word to anyone, including his brother, and drove away.

Felicia was next. She came over to me before she left.

"Good luck," I said.

"You'll do fine. Just follow Stan's lead and do what he says."

"I will."

She reached over and squeezed my hand and sent an erotic charge through me that I hadn't felt in years.

She walked out to her car, started it up, and backed down the driveway. As I watched her taillights disappear down the hill, I felt suddenly vulnerable, as if she'd taken my shelter in this new world with her.

Quiet Tom stared at me, his distrust and dislike mute but palpable.

Stan clapped him on the back. "What do you think, Thomas?"

Quiet Tom nodded.

Stan grinned. "Couldn't have said it better myself. Elliot?"

"Let's go," I said.

We went out to Tom's Armada, which he'd pulled up the driveway while we were gone. We loaded in with Tom driving, Stan up front, and me in the back.

We rode in silence. No small talk. No jokes. Stan was focused.

I was scared but less so than I could have ever predicted I would be. When the markers of one life have all fallen away, whatever rises to take their place becomes the new reality. I was scared of these men, scared of things going badly, scared of not seeing Felicia again, but I wasn't scared to be breaking the law. The morality by which I'd lived my whole life before that night seemed as trivial as the rules to some old board game. As we pulled into the hospital parking lot, I realized for the first time how little I'd actually believed in most of the laws which had governed my life up to that point.

We turned into the hospital campus and wound our way slowly to Elm Street, stopping twice to let patients and their families cross in front of us. Both times, the people gave Tom a polite wave of thanks. He waved back a *You're welcome*.

"Good," Stan said. "We're in no hurry here. Just three guys going to see a buddy in the hospital."

The parking lot adjacent to the Rockefeller Cancer Institute was about half full, with most of the cars parked in spaces closest to the doors. Tom stopped just beyond the patient unloading area, and Stan and I jumped out.

Tom turned right to pull into the parking lot. Stan and I ducked down the alley.

For twenty yards or more we crept through the dark. Just before the end of the alley the lights from the loading area slashed through the shadows, but before we reached the edge of the light, Stan pulled me into the short walkway of an emergency exit.

We pressed our backs to the building. The only thing I could hear, beyond the distant sound of tires on pavement, was my own breathing. I panted as if we'd just run.

Stan didn't seem to notice. I tried to watch for the truck, but Stan was more attuned to the loading dock.

The lot where the truck would pull past us and turn around was formed by the intersection of the backsides of three different buildings. As such, it was a rather small, misshapen triangle. We stood at the tip of the triangle by the entrance to the alley.

The unloading dock itself sat twenty-five yards away from us across the triangle. It was about five feet off the ground and thirty feet across. Wooden pallets sat stacked beside a sliding industrial door about ten feet wide. Stan watched that door intently but without my nervousness. In his left hand, he held a small disposable cell phone.

After a few minutes, the cell phone buzzed. A text popped up on the cheap blue screen: HERE.

He slid the phone in his pants pocket with his left hand and pulled a gun from his jacket with his right. It was an automatic of some kind with a silencer on the end that almost touched his knee when he held it by his side.

Adrenaline shot through me. Everything became real. I could smell grass and brick and mortar. Beads of sweat trickled down my chest. With that gun next to me in the dark, a terrible fear came over me. What if he killed the truck driver?

That thought seized me. What if Stan killed him? Just a man driving a truck for a living. A human being sitting in a truck right now with no idea that in a couple of minutes he would be killed …

I whispered, "You won't hurt the driver, right?"

"Shut up."

We heard the truck break near the entrance to the alley, heard it swing wide to turn in, saw high bright lights splash across the walls. Illumination barreled down the alleyway and lit up everything including us. Suddenly the eighteen-wheeler shot by in a whoosh of air and light and hulking mass.

Stan didn't tense up, didn't flinch. He must have known that in such a tight space the light from the truck would essentially light up the whole loading area. I hadn't known that, though, and I let out a gasp.

In the loading area, the driver swung hard to the right, jackknifed his trailer and expertly eased it back until it lined up perfectly with the dock. He did it without moving his elbow from his open window.

Stan ran.

I followed.

His gun disappeared. He darted low around the high, hot grill of the truck, swung up to the driver's side door, pushed a can of mace through the window and sprayed the man in the eyes. The driver was pale and pudgy, in his mid-thirties with shaggy brown hair and an unkempt goatee. Startled, he put his hands up. "What? No—o"

Stan opened the door and pushed himself inside.

I ran to the passenger side and fumbled up the steps to the door. It was locked—or at least, I couldn't open it—but

Stan opened it and swung it wide. I had to jump out of the way to avoid being smashed in the face by the door.

The driver yelled and began to jerk.

I grabbed one of his hands as Stan had instructed me earlier and clapped a handcuff on his wrist. He fought me.

"Please!" I said—the way you might snipe at an impatient child.

Stan elbowed the man in the throat. The man raised his hands to his neck.

"Now get his other hand," Stan said forcefully.

I struggled to get the man's wrist but the poor bastard was fighting not only me, but his crushed larynx, and the mace in his eyes, too. His hands were all over the place. I managed to get his second wrist clasped. Sweat covered my face. I wiped it away with my forearm, pulled the black cloth sack from my pocket and pulled it over his head.

Stan started up the truck.

"Easy," he said loud enough for us to hear. For a moment, I wasn't sure which one of us he was talking to. "Just stay calm and this will be over in a few moments."

He pushed the man's head into my lap.

"You just stay down," he shouted over the truck's roar, "and stay calm and you'll be done with this in a couple of minutes. You've been maced. It burns like hell. It causes temporary blindness." He popped the brake and we lurched forward up the alley. "But you will be okay. We are going to let you go. You're going to be okay in a matter of minutes. Your eyes will hurt for a little while, but you will be okay. Do you understand?"

"Yes," the man shouted.

I held his head in my lap.

Stan stopped at the end of the alley. A car with a father, mother and a couple of kids passed. An SUV filled with older women. Stan turned left. His driving wasn't as expert as the driver's had been, but it was good. You could tell he knew what he was doing. We crawled behind the SUV.

The man in my lap began to spasm. "My eyes," he cried.

Hands still on the wheel, Stan leaned over and shouted, "Shut up or I'll kill you." It was the first threat he'd used, and it worked. The man whimpered quietly.

At the stop sign, Stan turned left and gained speed as we headed for the interstate. We turned onto the interstate, gained more speed and joined the flow of traffic heading west.

The man in my lap whimpered and spasmed and clawed at his eyes through the hood, but he didn't cry out and he didn't vomit. I held him down, but I tried to do it without a sense of malice—like a parent holding down a screaming child at the doctor's office.

After a time, Stan signaled that he was pulling over to the side of the road. Traffic was fairly scarce and the place lay in darkness.

I opened my door and slid onto the top step of the truck. I started to pull the man out slowly to help him down, but Stan planted a foot in his back and kicked him out. He fell, slammed onto the ground, and rolled down a ditch into the dark.

"Let's go!" Stan shouted.

I swung back in and Stan pulled away.

* * *

The plan was to switch trucks. Our first stop was a little town just off of Interstate 40 called Fowler. We turned off the inter-state, took the two-lane service road a few miles, and pulled into the parking lot of a wholesale fence company. Stan drove to the back of the building, turned around and backed up through an open door into an enormous enclosed pole barn.

A few overhead lights illuminated the center section of the barn. Rolls of chain link and stacks of wrought iron and treated wood crowded three racks that climbed toward the roof. Waiting for us, Quiet Tom paced in a tight circle while Felicia leaned against the front of a cargo truck—probably thirty feet long—with ARKANSAS FENCE CO. painted on the side.

When we'd parked, she walked around to my side. As I climbed down she asked, "How'd it go?"

I couldn't think of what to say. I kept hearing that truck driver hit the ground. I just nodded.

She patted my arm, but she had already turned her attention to the truck.

"I didn't think the truck would be this big," she mumbled. "Where's Stan?"

We walked to the rear of the trailer.

The doors were open, and above us Stan stood inside, slouched against pallets of shrink wrapped boxes, reading the load's pink paper invoice. He was not smiling.

Felicia gasped. "What is it? Oh Jesus, Stan. Is it the wrong truck? Is it not the Oxy?"

"Oh, it's the Oxy, all right," he said, "but it's more than double the load. So instead of two million bucks worth of shit, I'd guesstimate we're sitting on about five million."

The Old Stuff 8

No one seemed happy about this seemingly good news.

Stan was mad because the plan had called for 80,000 units of Oxycodone, but it now appeared we had 200,000 units. For him it was a logistical nightmare. Though he didn't say it, I could tell he was also troubled by the simple fact that the information had been wrong. One flawed piece of information could mean mistakes in other areas.

Felicia seemed scared. She'd worked up just enough courage to steal two million dollars. The escalation to five million seemed to overwhelm her.

Quiet Tom said nothing, of course. But he'd been texting since we pulled up. I didn't think we'd have to wait long to see DB.

Among our little band of thieves, I had a unique perspective. I'd never loved money. When I was a preacher, I'd preached against such love—though that particular sermon never seemed to get a fair hearing because people naturally assume that greed is a sin of excess. Greed, they think, is wanting too much money. In reality, the problem with greed is that it prescribes an earthly remedy to a spiritual need, like giving salt water to a thirsty man. As I watched my new associates, it occurred to me that criminals like us were just stealing someone else's salt water. The trick, I could have told them, is that the contents of that truck were never going to make any of us happy.

Being the disgraced ex-preacher among a band of hijackers is a dubious position of moral authority, however, so I kept my observations to myself.

"What do we do?" Felicia asked.

Stan climbed down from the truck. Sweat dripped from his slicked back scarlet hair and fell down his bony face.

"We'll have to renegotiate the deal with the buyer."

Quiet Tom showed the readout of his cell phone to Stan.

"Nothing from the cops yet," Stan said. "Either the driver hasn't been found, or it hasn't been reported. That luck won't last much longer. He'll scramble to the top of the ditch and someone will stop."

"How much time do we have?" Felicia asked.

"None," Stan said. "We should assume it's already happened. So we proceed as planned: First we unload the shit. We'll fill the switch truck and stack the rest here. We can hide it here. Then we ditch the big truck."

He clapped, and we got to work. Quiet Tom pulled out the ramps on both the trucks, while Stan produced two pallet jacks. He worked one, and Tom worked the other. They jacked up a pallet and pulled it while either Felicia or I pushed from the other side and helped to steer and stabilize. We moved quickly and had the switch truck full in a matter of minutes.

Quiet Tom disappeared around a corner and then reappeared a moment later driving a large, loud contraption that looked like the bastard offspring of a combine harvester and a fork lift. It was yellow and black with four-foot high tires and a huge hydraulic lift. He operated it with as much skillful ease as the truck driver had guided his tractor trailer. In a few moments he'd stashed the remaining pallets on the highest rack of the warehouse, well out of sight of a casual observer.

"He does that well," I said.

Felicia wiped sweat from her face with a small handkerchief. "He owns the place," she said.

"He does?"

"Arkansas Fencing Company," she said. She leaned close to my ear. "On the verge of bankruptcy."

"Ah," I said.

After we were done, Stan climbed into the stolen truck. "Elliot, you're with me. Tom you're here. Felicia, you follow us in the Armada."

We all scurried to our assignments. In just a few minutes Stan and I hit the service road and for the first time since the robbery had begun I felt a real, gut-level fear. Committing a crime, I'd discovered, wasn't that scary. Trying to get away with it, however, was terrifying.

Beside me, very softly, Stan began to whistle the hymn "Are You Washed in the Blood of the Lamb?"

I almost laughed. Was he pretending to be at ease? Trying to sooth his jittery apprentice? Was he just messing with me?

Then in a startling voice—high and clear like a fine bluegrass singer—Stan sang:

> *"Are you washed in the blood,*

In the soul-cleansing blood of the lamb?

Are your garments spotless? Are they white as snow?

Are you washed in the blood of the lamb?"

He sighed. "Those old church songs, they're so beautiful. Don't you think so? I hate that new stuff they play today. The old hymns really said something. About heaven and hell. About transgression and sin."

"Yes ..."

"Did you play the old stuff when you were a preacher or did you do the new stuff?"

"You want to talk about this now?"

"Would you rather sit there and worry?"

My nerves settled a bit as I tried to formulate a response. "We did a mix. I like the old stuff better myself, but a lot of people like the contemporary Christian. So we'd alternate it."

Stan shook his head. "Tells you all you need to know about our country that the word 'contemporary' is just another way of saying 'shitty.'"

"I guess."

"Whole damn point of religion is that it's old. There's nothing new under the sun—that's scripture, ain't it?"

"Ecclesiastes."

"What?"

"The, uh, the book of Ecclesiastes. 'What has been will be again. What has been done will be done again. There is nothing new under the sun.'"

Stan smiled at that, but he was quiet for a while. Finally he said, "A scripture quoting heist man. That's fucking beautiful."

We arrived at our drop off point, the parking lot behind a bus factory in another town just off the interstate. Stan parked, and I got out. He ignited a gallon milk-jug full of gasoline in the cab, tossed another into the trailer, and we got into Felicia's car and left as the truck went up in flames. We were on I-40 in less than one minute, heading back to the fence company.

When we pulled in, DB was waiting with his brother. They huddled together next to the SUV in the warehouse.

As soon as Felicia parked, DB broke away from his brother and rushed to us. When Stan opened his door, DB said, "We need to get this shit out of here."

"What's the latest?"

"There is no latest."

Stan frowned. "They haven't found the driver yet?"

"No!"

Stan leaned against the SUV and pondered that a second. "That's damn peculiar." He turned to me. "You see that guy get up after we pushed him out of the truck?"

"No."

"Hmm. Maybe he hit the ground at a funny angle."

That made me dizzy. I reached out and steadied myself on the SUV.

DB said, "Either way, he'll be reported as soon as the hospital calls whoever they call to complain that the shipment didn't come in."

"No telling when that will be," Stan said.

"I don't care when it is," DB said. "We need to get this shit out of here." He pointed at the top rack. "I don't know why you stashed that stuff up there."

"We might need to store it," Stan said.

DB shook his head violently. "Won't work."

Felicia said, "Not to interrupt, but is there a bathroom?"

Stan said, "That's not a bad idea. We could use some food, too."

DB said, "We don't have time—"

"Until I talk to Fuller," Stan said, "we don't have anywhere to go. We need to call him and bring him up to date and see if he can pony up the extra three million for all the excess shipment."

DB wanted to argue, but his brother touched his arm and seemed to calm him. He motioned up the road running behind the building.

"Okay," DB said. "Let's go up the house."

Chief Among Sinners 9

The twins lived a few miles from the Arkansas Fence Company along a two-lane road. We passed quiet houses and fallow fields, and pulled into the driveway of a one-story brick home with an oak tree in the front yard. Quiet Tom led us inside. The house had brown carpet and striped wallpaper that dated from the late seventies or early eighties. Family pictures hung on the wall over a worn sofa. The twins took after their stout, sour-faced mother. Their scrawny father had buckteeth and thick glasses.

Felicia hit the bathroom. Stan went onto a small back patio and made a phone call. The twins dug some leftovers out of the refrigerator.

I used the bathroom next. Its decor was lighthouse and nautical-themed. I pissed while staring at a figurine of an old sea captain. When I was done, I washed my hands, and there, over the sink, was Elliot Stilling in the mirror.

He looked rough, this new Elliot. Tired, dirty. He'd helped steal a truck. A man might be dead because of him.

Oh Jesus, please no!

When you're a born again Christian, you teach yourself to listen for God in your own thoughts. You teach yourself to interpret your feelings and fears and desires as promptings of the Holy Spirit or tricks of Satan. It had been almost two years since I had been brutally relieved of the impression that God was listening to me. But like a grown man crying for his mother, some part of me cried out for Jesus to help me.

But I wasn't a child. I was a man. If that driver was dead, he was dead. Crying to God would have no effect on it one way or another. God lets everybody die.

When I walked out, Felicia was eating some cold pizza. She said, "You get the sense their mother decorated this place and they never saw fit to change it?"

I nodded.

The twins sat in the living room signing back and forth, ignoring the rest of us.

Stan walked in. "We'll have to wait."

DB stood up. "We've decided we can't wait."

"Who's we?"

"Me and my brother. We can't wait."

"Gonna have to," Stan said.

"Why?"

"Because we need to meet with Fuller to discuss the money, that's why."

DB shook his head. "My brother and me got millions of dollars worth of stolen drugs sitting down there in our fucking warehouse."

"Any reason why the cops would look there?" Stan asked.

"No, but that don't make me feel any more secure."

"What would you like to do, DB? Where would you like to take the fortune in stolen pharmaceuticals sitting down there in your warehouse?"

DB grasped for something to say to that.

Stan said, "You don't have any ideas. Of course not. So why don't you calm down. I've arranged a meeting with Fuller. With any luck, he'll be able to take the stuff off our hands tonight. Until then, just relax."

"How the hell am I supposed to do that?"

"Sit. Breath. Stop talking."

With hardly more dignity than a petulant child, DB slumped down in an easy chair by the kitchen doorway. Tom—apparently unable to watch his brother capitulate — jumped up and stalked into the kitchen. DB sulked.

Felicia and I sat down on the sofa.

Stan plopped into the love seat under a large picture frame window looking out on the short driveway. He grinned at DB's obvious displeasure. "Did I tell you that Elliot here used to be a preacher?"

"A preacher?"

Stan nodded.

"How come he ain't a preacher no more?"

"Excellent question. Been wondering that myself. Elliot?"

I rubbed my palms together. Felicia examined her hands, but I could tell by the tension in her shoulders that she was interested in the answer, too.

"I quit," I said.

"Obviously," Stan said. "How come, though?"

Felicia looked up at me.

"Life," I told her.

Stan massaged his cardinal-colored tie between his thumb and forefinger. "Come on. You have a better answer than that. You were a preacher. God's humble servant here on earth. A shepherd amongst the sheep. How could you turn your back on your calling?"

Felicia said, "Leave him alone, Stan."

Stan smiled. "How sweet." He asked me, "So, am I permitted to inquire if you were married, Brother Stilling?"

"Yes," I said. I nudged the nasty old carpet with the toe of my shoe. "I was."

Felicia said, "Leave him alone, Stan. He doesn't want to talk about it with you."

Stan watched her for a moment with no expression on his face. Then he asked me, "You met our sad-eyed angel here at the hospital. Why were you there?"

"I tried to kill myself."

His face brightened. I seemed to delight him in the same way that new facts delight a scholar. "Now why did you go and do that?"

"I was depressed."

Stan had a way of staring at you like a scientist taking something apart. "But what finally sent you over the edge?" he asked.

I shook my head.

I dropped the phone and ran. Out my office door, down the hall, down the steps.

My car was parked in my usual space. Right where I'd left it. Tree limbs bent in the wind and leaves slapped at a sky drained of color.

"Don't know or won't say," Stan inquired.

"Won't say."

Stan wasn't impressed by my sudden infusion of defiance, but he did keep smiling.

"Must have been bad," he said. "You tried to kill yourself over it."

"Didn't just try. Succeeded. I was dead for a few minutes."

"Three minutes," Felicia offered.

"You met Felicia then, what, as she was dragging you back into this world?"

"Something like that," I said.

"And now here you are. Hooked up with Felicia and her ragtag band of desperados. Felicia brought you back to life and now she's got you heisting trucks." He sat back and crossed his legs and laced his long fingers together over one bony knee.

Felicia sunk into the sagging sofa cushions.

"I guess," I said. "But I chose to be here. At this point, I don't know what the alternative could be."

"You can't repent of your sins, go back to God?"

"God and I are done."

"And here you are. Doesn't seem like a good trade off."

I shrugged. "Without God, there's no wall between us and the dark."

Stan's usually quick retort seemed stunted this time. He glared at me. "What?"

"Something I used to use in my sermons." I waved it away. "My father said it once."

Stan's face had flushed. His smile and his causal, playful manner were gone. For just a moment, he didn't even seem dangerous. "I like the way your father thinks."

DB groaned, "C'mon Stan, not this Jesus shit again."

Stan ignored him and asked me, "What did your father say about your suicide attempt?"

I shook my head. "He's dead. Died a few years ago."

"So he never knew about your suicide."

"No."

"Unless, of course, he's in heaven watching over you."

"I guess."

"And do you think he is?"

"In heaven watching over me?"

"Yeah."

"If there's a heaven."

Stan smiled. "But is there a heaven?"

DB sat up in the recliner. "Is this what we're here to talk about?"

"Shut up," Stan snapped at him. Then to me, "Is there?"

DB jumped to his feet and darted toward the doorway to the dining room. "This is a waste of time! We need to—"

"We're waiting on Fuller," Stan told him.

"You should call Fuller back. Try to do it on the phone."

"That's an idiotic idea."

"Well, I think you should get aggressive with him. Tell him you want the cash and the truck pronto. He's gonna want it. There's no reason to wait for a face-to-face."

Quiet Tom appeared in the doorway. He signed something to his brother.

"Good idea," DB said. "Maybe I should call Fuller myself."

"Do you have his number?"

"No, but you could give it to me."

"And why would I do that?" Stan asked.

"Why not?"

Stan drew his gun and placed it on the cushion beside him. In a calm voice he said, "Because I'm in charge. Because you're an imbecile. Because neither you nor your imbecilic brother could have pulled off a heist of this size and complexity without me. But mostly, DB, just because. Just because I said so."

DB swayed a bit, his eyes on the gun.

Blood beat in my ears.

Tom pulled at his brother's arm. DB backed up, still keeping an eye on the gun.

They retreated through the dining room and into the kitchen.

Stan watched them leave. Then he turned to me. His sharp face was pale again, but his smile was gone. "Well?" he said. "Is there a heaven?"

"I—I don't ... I don't know, Stan."

Felicia let out the breath she'd been holding. "Are they going to be ..."

Stan waved that away. He asked me, "So you're saying your father might not be in heaven?"

"I suppose that's what I'm saying."

"Then what happened to your father when he died?"

"I don't know. Nothing, I guess."

"And that's that," Stan said.

"I suppose so."

I thought I could hear the brothers signing to each other in the next room—though perhaps I just imagined it because it seemed impossible that they weren't in there furiously discussing what had just happened.

Stan picked up his gun and tapped it against his knee as absently as a pair of glasses. "Given how I was brought up,

I ain't known that many self-proclaimed atheists in my life. A couple, but not many. Believe it or not even in the, ah, *criminal underworld* most folks tend to believe in God."

Felicia told him, "It's weird that you always want to talk about this stuff. Do you know that it's weird?"

"How come?"

"You talk like a Jesus freak, but then you turn around and act like you."

Stan put down the gun. He crossed his arms and extended his long legs. "Jesus suffered for our sins," he explained. "I've sinned a lot, so I guess Jesus suffered a lot for my sins. I like to think that when he was out there bleeding to death in the brutal desert sun, he was thinking of me." He tilted his head in genuine bemusement. "I'm surprised everyone don't feel the same."

I leaned up. "Doesn't she have a point though?"

"About what?"

The gun beside him on the cushion stared at me like a third eye.

"Nothing," I said.

"No. Come on. I'm used to scraping together conversation with those degenerates in the next room. When a man takes these things seriously, he lives to find another man who takes them seriously, too. Ask me what you want to ask me."

"Okay. Well, isn't there a disparity between the way you live and your interest in religion?"

"You saying I'm a hypocrite?" he asked flatly.

Rubbing my slick palms together I said, "No. No. I just—"

"No, it's okay," he said. "But that's what you're both getting at, right?"

I was too afraid to reply to that.

Stan said, "It goes back a-ways with me. When I was a kid, this old man used to take me to church. My parents had both run off and this old man took me in. He worked me like a slave, but he fed me and took me to church. And I mean this church was *waaay* back in the Ozarks, back where they preach that real washed-in-the-blood country shit.

"The preacher was fat and sweaty and a real screamer. He'd get all worked up and sweat and scream and everyone would go down to the altar and pray and holler and roll around. Me, I never did. The preacher would yell at me, cast Satan out of me in the name of Jesus, beg the Holy Ghost to fill me up so I could speak in tongues and get saved. But it never happened; I never got a in-filling of the Holy Ghost. They all worried about me, but I knew why it didn't happen. I didn't want it to. Not yet.

"I'd done my scripture reading, and I'd seen where Apostle Paul said he was the chief among the sinners." He paused. "You know that verse?"

"Yes."

"What is it, chapter and verse?"

"It's ... First Timothy."

"Yes ..."

"One-fifteen, I think."

"Well done! Exactly right, First Timothy 1:15. I'd read that verse and I'd pondered it. If Apostle Paul was bragging that he was the chief sinner, well then what he was really saying was that Jesus had died the most for him. Right? If Jesus died for our sins and Apostle Paul was the chief sinner, then hell, he had the most glorious salvation. And me, what had I done? Nothin', that's what. All my sinning was the sinning of a little boy. Telling white lies and thinking bad thoughts. Why make Jesus Christ hang on the cross for that? For the thoughts of a child?

"When I figured that out, I knew what I had to do. I knew then I wasn't gonna go down there and roll around with that bunch of screamin' hillbillies until I'd done some serious fucking transgressing first. Apostle Paul *earned* his glorious salvation by being the chief sinner. I figure to outdo him.

"First I run off and joined the Marines. I suspected I could do some real sinning there, and I was correct. They sent me to the desert to kill some sand-niggers. I went and killed some, but then after a while they said I was too intense and they kicked me out." He sat up and draped one skinny knee over the other. "So like that," he snapped his fingers, "my military career was over. They shipped me back to the states, California of all places. There was nobody out there worth talking to, so I come back to Arkansas."

Stan turned his head toward the doorway.

He picked up the gun.

"When I got back to Arkansas," he said, "I started on my path. Since there wasn't no way to achieve a true breakthrough on the right side of the law, I started my criminal career. I never told no one about my plan, of course. They just figured I was another cracker-ass hillbilly gangster. But I been chipping away at it day after day for years now, accruing all the sinning I can.

"That revelation I had reading scripture, that was a message from God. He wanted me to see the nothing at the bottom of everything and the everything at the bottom of nothing. The greater the sin, the greater the salvation."

"But how long?" I asked. "How long do you have to go until you're ready?"

Stan grimaced. "That is a damn fine question. I figure since Jesus got baptized at thirty-two, I'll do it then."

Felicia shook her head. "You are truly fucking crazy, Stan."

"You're a sinner because you're too lazy and stupid to be anything else," Stan snapped. "You shouldn't assume the same thing is true of me. I could be pure as milk if that's what God had in mind. But he set me on a different course."

He leaned back. He placed the gun in his lap. "What about you, Elliot? What do you think of my story?"

"I understand it."

"Is that a fact?" he said.

"I killed myself. I think I know about the nothing at the bottom of everything."

Stan searched my face like he was taking a good look in a mirror.

In the kitchen, the brothers were moving around again. Felicia craned her neck to look through the doorway, but Stan was waiting for me to continue.

I said, "You're saying that it's a choice between God or nothing at all."

"Yes," he said.

"And to embrace the one you have to embrace the other. Because without sin, there can be no salvation."

"The darkness that gives meaning to the light," he said.

Felicia looked me and opened her mouth, but she didn't say anything.

Stan said, "Nobody's ever gotten that before."

"What do you suppose it means that I'm the first?" I asked.

"I don't know yet."

"Could be worth thinking about," I said.

"It is worth thinking about," Stan said. Then he grimaced. "Isn't it, boys?"

I turned as the brothers walked into the room.

DB leveled his gun at Stan. "I don't care what it means," he said. "I'm here for the goddamn money."

Dirty Work 10

Stan's eyes darted back and forth between the brothers. Quiet Tom, clutching a butcher knife, strode to the left to cover Felicia and me. DB positioned himself almost at the center of the room in a shooter's stance, legs apart, left arm bent in support of the gun hand. His head was tilted to the side in order to line up the site of his gun with Stan's forehead.

Stan said, "I take it you're not pleased with my leadership." I couldn't see his gun, and I wasn't sure where he'd moved it.

"You just keep your hands on your knees," DB said. "I'm going to give you my handcuffs, and you're going to cuff yourself. Then you'll call Fuller and we'll negotiate the money and a new truck. I didn't get involved in this mess so you could waste time debating religion and then turn around and call me stupid."

"Fuller doesn't do bidness over the phone," Stan said. "What will calling him accomplish?" His face looked nearly bored.

"Plenty."

"Like what?" Stan asked.

DB blinked away a bead of sweat. "Just—"

Stan shot him three times in the chest. The shots were small, metallic claps, and the bullets poked three red holes in DB's T-shirt. He got off one booming shot that shattered the window above Stan's head, and then his hands dropped to his sides. His gun hit the floor with a thud. He dropped to his knees like he was going to pray and fell forward and slammed his face into the carpet. His knees were still bent. Except for the bloody triangle between his shoulder blades, he looked like he was doing yoga.

Stan raised his gun to Quiet Tom. Shock spread over the twin's face. No one made a sound until he opened his mouth, but it took a second or two for something to come out.

It was an awful high-pitched moan.

"The knife," Stan said.

Tom dropped the knife.

"Floor's getting cluttered," Stan said.

Tom cried out again, his skin stretched tight against his skull.

Stan watched him like he watched everything else, like poor Tom was part of an experiment he was conducting with the human race. He didn't flinch when Tom began to cry, his hold on things disintegrating by the millisecond.

"Du-ane!" Tom groaned.

Stan shot him once in the chest.

Felicia yelped when the stocky little man staggered forward. He tripped on his brother's arm and stumbled to the floor.

But he wasn't dead. Somehow he managed to climb to a knee. His chest wasn't bleeding yet, but his face was already white. Stan lifted the gun and shot him in the forehead. This time the twin dropped, his legs intertwined with his brother's arm in a pool of blood, and he hit the floor. His bloody back rose as the last breath left his body.

I slunk to the carpet. Felicia scrambled onto the sofa as if water were rising in the room.

Stan stood up. Blood flecked his face and his dirty white suit, but he had killed the brothers without leaving his chair.

He stared at them a moment. Then he said, "Tom didn't die very stoically, did he?"

I blinked up at him a few times.

Stan said, "Then again, I guess it's hard to be stoic when you're dying for nothing." The gun hung at his side as he looked at Felicia. "It's over now. You going to be able to compose yourself?"

She nodded.

"What about you?" he asked me.

I blinked and looked at the brothers. "They're dead," I said.

He regarded the dead men. "Yeah," he said. "They weren't much help to begin with, but DB's connection with the department was useful." He frowned. "Necessary, even. I didn't particularly want to do that, but they didn't give me much choice."

"They're dead," Felicia said.

Stan looked at her, then at me. "You two are in shock." His mouth twisted to one side. "Which I understand. Still, you need to pull yourselves together so we can get rid of the brothers grim here." He walked over to Felicia and put his hand under her chin. "You listening?"

Felicia had been around enough death that she quickly started recouping her senses. She pulled away from him and said, "Okay, Stan. Jesus. Just be calm." She ran her hands through her hair. "Just be calm."

Stan held out his hand for her to see its steadiness. "I'm as peaceful as early morning, darlin'. You might want to look to your boyfriend, though."

Felicia stood up slowly and her legs wobbled, but she got to me and put her hand under my chin. "Are you okay?"

I couldn't say anything yet. I just looked at the dead men's blood seeping into the carpet. There was a stillness in the twins more frightening than any movement could ever be. They meant nothing to me, and during the short time I'd known them, they'd only inspired fear in me, but just a few minutes before, they had been unmistakably alive. Now they were unmistakably not.

Felicia lifted my face to hers. Her hands were cold and her left eye was bloody up close. But both of her eyes had the same message: *Pull yourself together or we are going to die on this floor.*

"Are you okay?" she asked.

"Yes."

"Are you sure?"

"Yes." I patted her arm.

"Good," Stan said. "Now both of you get up."

Felicia took my arm and guided me to my feet. She clutched my arm as if she were drowning—and her voice trembled when she asked Stan, "What now?"—but she was the only thing holding me up.

Stan slipped his gun beneath his coat. He clapped his hands.

"We need to get rid of these boys. First, Felicia, you go to the bathroom and take down the shower curtain and the liner. Fold them together. Then go get the curtain and the liner from the bathroom at the other end of the house. Bring all of it in here."

"There are two bathrooms?" she asked.

"Yes." He pointed down a short hallway to the left. "DB's room is that way. Used to be his parents' master bed and bath." To the right: "Guest room and Tom's room. Guest bath. Remember curtain and liner from both."

She patted my arm. "Okay?"

I nodded, still blinking.

She let go of my arm, but before she took a step, Stan stopped her. His face nearly touched hers when he told her, "The twins are dead. You deal with enough death you should be able to hold yourself together and think clearly."

She nodded. "I am thinking clearly."

"Good. You keep yourself together and the three of us will make some serious money. On the other side of it, though, this just turned into a murder rap."

"I understand," she said. Her voice was steady.

Stan looked at me. "What about you, Elliot?"

I nodded. "I understand."

Stan jerked his head toward the door. "Get moving, Felicia."

She patted my arm again and left. Stan didn't stop looking at me. I glanced down at the twins. There was a hole in the back of Tom's head, and I saw bloody fragments of his brain on his shoulder. I put my hand to my mouth, though I didn't feel any kind of nausea. Too stunned for horror, I simply stared at him, taken aback at the sight of the inside on the outside.

"First time with this kind of thing?" Stan asked.

From the bathroom, I could hear Felicia climb into the tub to take down the shower curtain.

"Ever seen a dead body?" he asked.

IdropthephoneandrunOutmyofficedownthehalldownthe stepsMycarparkedinmyusualspaceRightwhereIleftit

"I've seen my share," I said.

"Not piled up on the floor, though," Stan said.

"No," I said. I dropped my hand from my mouth. "Not piled up on the floor."

He nodded and regarded the twins with something close to sadness. "What a world." He sucked in his bottom lip.

Felicia crossed the hall with plastic in her hands. "No curtain down there, just a liner. I'll check in this one."

"May I go to the door to get some air?" I asked.

"Sure," he said. "Just don't go outside."

I walked to the sliding back door, pulled it open and stuck my head out. The humid air, thick with the smell of sap and damp leaves, wasn't exactly refreshing, but it was something. A few weak stars glimmered in the canopy of darkness spread over the house, and from the trees night life rustled and chirped and croaked. The world seemed alive.

As I pulled my head back in, Felicia walked into the room with the plastic shower liners folded under her arm. The room still smelled of Stan's gunpowder.

"Are you okay?" she asked me.

"Yes," I said. "Air."

Stan took the liners from Felicia and gestured for her to stand by me. She was shaking. I didn't realize why until she asked Stan, "Are you going to kill us?"

Stan's brow furrowed as if she'd insulted him. "Why would I kill you?"

"I don't know," she said.

"I'm not some psycho, Felicia. The man had a gun pointed at me. What was I supposed to do? Talk things over?"

"I guess not," she said. "I'm sorry. I'm just scared."

"Fair enough," Stan said. "Now take off your clothes."

I was still in shock. I couldn't think about much except the men at our feet bleeding into the carpet. I'd been dead the day before. And Stan still had a gun.

But Felicia had bundled up whatever she felt and stuck it somewhere it wouldn't distract her. "What do you mean?" she asked Stan.

"The two of you need to carry these corpses," Stan explained. "It will be a messy job and, as you will need your clothes later on, you'll have to do this work naked."

"We could wear some ... clothes," Felicia said. "Burn them later or something."

Stan shook his head. "No," he said. "There's no use bloodying more clothes. Just more potential evidence."

Felicia was silent.

Stan smirked. "It's nothing I haven't seen before," he told her.

She turned to me and looked in my eyes. "Take off your clothes," she said.

I felt almost drunk. There was none of the euphoria of drunkenness, of course, but there was the same slowing thickness. I unbuttoned my shirt, my fingers useless like Styrofoam. Beside me, Felicia locked eyes with Stan and pulled off her tank-top. Her wine-colored bra made her skin look pale. She kicked off her shoes and took off her jeans. Her underwear was the color of wine, too. I watched her.

Stan said, "Shock or no shock, he still wants to look at you naked. Isn't that funny?"

"Hilarious," Felicia said and took off her bra and panties. She folded her clothes and left them on the love seat. I looked at her and she let me look, figuring perhaps the time for modesty was past, or perhaps she just thought it made sense to let me get the look over with.

She was pale. Her breasts were small and her stomach soft. Her legs were skinny and dotted here and there with yellow bruises. I watched her move and it seemed as if we were both moving in water.

"Okay," Stan said. "Get him up and at it."

Felicia took my face in her hands and peeled my eyelids back with the tips of her fingers.

"He's still in shock," she said.

"Get him unshocked," Stan said.

"That's not the way it works," Felicia said, but she jostled me and said, "You in there? Say something to me."

"Hello," I said.

"Hello," she replied. "Let's get your clothes off."

With her help, I took off my clothes. My body was paler and softer than hers, my dick shrunken to the size of a packing peanut. I closed my eyes and reopened them. It was like I was waking up from a long sleep.

Stan dropped the shower liners on the floor and gestured at the twins. "Now put Tom there on one of these."

Felicia pulled me toward the bodies and stepped over Tom. She took a shower liner and opened it up. I bent down.

"Roll him," she told me. "Don't try lifting him. Don't look at his head. Just think about the job. Help me roll him."

I took his forearm. It was bloody and still warm. Ignoring the blood, I tightened my grip and pulled him toward the shower curtain. I didn't look at the hole in the back of his head or the bits of mushroom-colored brain on his shirt. I didn't think about the gross smoothness of his skin, how it was hairy and too soft. I didn't think about the dead man I was touching. I concentrated on the job.

We had some difficulty pulling him to the center of the liner because the plastic kept bunching up in his left armpit, yet we managed. Felicia covered him with the ends of the curtain.

"Now the other one," Stan said.

Felicia spread out the second liner, and we took DB by the arms and legs and turned him over, but his eyes and mouth were open. I fell back onto the carpet.

Stan grimaced.

"It's okay," Felicia told me. "It happens. It's okay. Let's just do this. Don't look at it."

I picked myself up and crawled back over.

"Christ," I said.

She said, "It's good that you're jolted," she said.

"Jesus," I said. I wiped sweat from my face and noticed blood on my hands. "Jesus."

We rolled DB over. I didn't look at his face. When Felicia covered him up, I took a deep breath and looked up at Stan.

He stood by the door, legs spread, arms folded across his chest, and watched us without the benefit of mercy. It was impossible to know what he was thinking. Maybe about the task at hand. Maybe about God. Maybe nothing.

"Pick up Tom," he told us. "Carry him to the bathroom. First, fold the ends of the curtain so no blood drips out."

We did as we were told, but the body slumped in the middle, like a hinge snapping shut. It dropped to the floor.

"Turn him over," Stan instructed. "Carry him upside down so he's facing the floor. It'll keep him from buckling up like that. When you get him to the bathroom, put him in the tub with his head facing the drain."

Felicia and I folded the ends of the plastic again and turned the body over.

"Carry him at the knees, Felicia," Stan said.

We lifted the body. He was short, but he was thick. Stan backed out of the way. We shuffled forward with the body and moved into the brown-paneled hallway. I heard my teeth chattering and clamped my mouth shut. We moved into the bathroom where the linoleum was cold. Without Stan saying anything more, we lowered Tom into the bathtub, his head against the silver faucet. Then, we went back to get DB. We folded the curtain, turned him over and lifted him as we had his brother. We lay DB on top of his brother.

"Both of you stay in there," Stan said.

We stood side by side, Felicia's skin touching mine. There was nothing sexual in it, but there was something primal. As we stood there blinking at Stan, waiting for the horror of our situation to sink to the next level, it felt as if she were part of me.

"Turn on the shower," Stan said. "Warm and on low, and make sure the drain is open."

I reached over and switched on the shower. The showerhead spat out water that bounced off the dead men like a waterfall hitting rocks. In seconds, the spray covered me. It was freezing, but it cleared my head a little. Felicia didn't pay any attention to the water. Glaring at Stan, she asked, "What now?"

"Unwrap them. Rinse off the liners and put them in the sink."

Unwrapping the bodies was a chore, especially Tom because he was on bottom, but eventually I pulled the liners clear of the dead men, let the shower rinse the blood and specks of skin and brain off, and then stuck them in the sink.

Stan handed Felicia Tom's butcher knife. I had not noticed Stan picking it up.

Felicia took the knife with a trembling hand. "What?" she asked in a small voice. "What do you want me to do?"

"Cut off their clothes. Cut away from your hand."

Felicia seemed relieved. She knelt down on the blue bathmat and ran the knife under DB's blood-soaked T-shirt and sliced it off of him. She unbuckled his belt and sliced open his pants and boxers. Then she did the same with Tom, peeling the clothes off of the dead men like layers of skin. Then she pulled off their shoes and socks.

"Reach under the sink there, Elliot," Stan said, as casually as if we were grouting the bathroom tile. "See if there's a trashcan with a plastic liner."

I opened the cabinet under the sink and pulled out a small wastebasket. It was empty and lined with a blue plastic Walmart shopping bag.

"Put the clothes in the bag," he said.

I pulled the bag out and stuffed the sopping clothes into it.

Stan nodded to himself and muttered, "Should have waited until they were out of their clothes to turn on the water. Live and learn."

"The shoes won't fit," I told him.

"Put them in the trashcan," he said. "It's all going in a larger trash bag later, anyway."

Beside me, Felicia was curled up, covering herself. She set down the knife.

"Not yet, dear," Stan said.

Felicia stared hard at him. "What?"

"We need to drain them."

"What do you mean?"

"Cut their throats open and let that gallon or so of blood slopping around in them leak out."

Felicia shook her head. "Please," she said. "Please, Stan. They've already bled a lot."

"They're going to bleed a lot more. Better to do it here before we move them."

She looked at the knife, slick and shining, lying on the floor.

"You always wanted to be a doctor," Stan said. "Here's your chance. Think of it as surgery."

Felicia closed her eyes. "Please," she said. Under the cold current of the shower and the gurgling of water down the drain, her voice was just a whisper.

Stan stood there, as inarguable as nature, and stared down at her.

When she opened her eyes, she raised them to him for just a moment, saw what the situation was, took a deep breath and picked up the knife. Then she turned to me and said, "I'm so sorry I got you into this."

I shook my head. "You can do this," I told her. "Think of it as a job. Think of it as surgery like he said."

She nodded and leaned into the tub. I didn't want to watch, but I didn't want make her do it alone. I leaned into the cold mist with her. Water bounced off the naked bodies and spit in our faces.

"The jugular," she told me. "That's what we need. It and the carotid are right next to each other."

She pushed the twin's head to the left side with the heel of her hand. When she sunk in the knife just above his collarbone on the right side, blood seeped out around the blade and ran down the twin's neck and face in rivulets with the shower water. One of his eyelids had opened when we unwrapped him, and his eye—yellow and dead and bubbled with fat water droplets—stared at the wall, but his slacked mouth and bloodied teeth didn't flinch.

I had to turn away. Next to me, Felicia's shoulder blades shifted beneath her pale skin as she worked. After a moment, she dropped the knife in the tub and rinsed her hands in the shower. She slumped against the tub, her blue lips trembling, her clean wet fists tight against her abdomen. She started to cry.

We lay there, naked and shivering, Stan watching us like a prison guard in some special hell. Behind us, the water rained down on the brothers and washed away their blood like mud.

Stan had the oddest look on his face—understanding, almost sad. He said, "It's enough to make you think God has turned his face away from us completely, isn't it?"

Divisions of Labor 11

When Stan felt enough time had passed, we pulled the twins out of the tub one at a time and wrapped them in the shower liners. We bundled the packages with duct tape Stan found in the garage and laid them side by side in the hallway. Then he instructed us to shower.

Felicia went first, turning the water to hot, and washing herself with soap and shampoo. I didn't watch her. I sat naked on the floor, legs against my chest, and shivered. When I looked up at all, it was to watch Stan watching her, a frown on his face. I didn't know what he was thinking or feeling. It's possible he was feeling nothing at all, though I doubt it. I'd dealt with enough screwed up people trying to project detachment; I knew what it looked like. Stan the Man was cold-blooded, but he was human. He was feeling something in there. Some signal from his conscience twisted up through his wiring and bothered him.

Maybe.

Or maybe he was simply planning what to do next. When Felicia finished, he handed her a towel and nodded at me.

"Your turn."

I climbed in and eased the hot water up. It ran over my body like water over ice, and I felt as if I were melting beneath it.

I washed, the lather dripping down my hands pink with blood. Felicia wrapped the towel around her chest and sat down on the toilet lid.

After I'd rinsed my hair, Stan said, "Enough."

I shut off the water, and he threw me a towel.

"We'll go in the bedroom. You'll get dressed, and then we'll take the boys for a ride."

While Stan moved the Armada, I followed Felicia through the hallway and into the bedroom. We dressed in silence, without looking at each other. My clothes stuck to my chest and arms because I hadn't properly dried off. Felicia's hair dripped on her shoulders.

When we came out, Stan pointed at the bodies. "One at a time out the front. Elliot, you carry the upper body and Felicia carries the legs."

We did as we were told. We turned off the front porch light and Stan waited beside the Armada in the dark as we carried out the first body. I wasn't sure which body was which anymore. I didn't think about it, didn't think at all about the dead man wrapped in plastic. I just concentrated on not dropping him.

We crowded around the back of the SUV. Stan lowered the tailgate and lifted the hatch. He pushed down the seats in the third row. Felicia and I struggled to hoist the body into it, and Stan stood behind me, watching.

We pushed the stiffening body into the storage space.

"One more time," Stan said.

"Thanks for the help," Felicia grumbled.

"I kill 'em, you carry 'em," Stan said. "Division of labor."

We trudged back up the stairs. Felicia and I sweated. Stan hummed the hymn, "Bringing in the Sheaves." We lifted the body, carried it down the stairs as we had before, and lugged it into the garage.

"Is there going to be space?" Felicia asked.

Stan smiled. "It's supposed to seat eight comfortably. I'm sure it will accommodate a couple of dead guys."

And it did. We lowered the second man onto his brother, and Stan covered them with a dirty, blue tarp he found in the garage. When he dropped the hatchback, I felt as if the brothers had been loaded into a hearse.

* * *

I drove. Felicia sat beside me, and Stan sat behind her. When I pulled onto the blacktop I asked, "Where are we going?"

"Go back to the interstate and head north," Stan answered.

For the first time, I noticed the moon bright above the scraps of gray clouds littering the night sky. I thought of the dead men in the back, thought of the moon resuscitating them like zombies in a horror movie, giving life to them like the sun gives life to trees and flowers.

I pulled onto I-40 North. Felicia sat beside me sucking her bottom lip.

She turned to me. "What?" she asked.

"Nothing," I said.

I glanced back at Stan. He watched me, and it didn't seem as if he were simply sitting. He seemed both relaxed and perched at the same time. He stared at me.

"Go the speed limit," he said. "Nobody wants to get pulled over."

I hadn't realized I was speeding, but I was cruising along at about 85 miles an hour. I pulled it back down to the speed limit.

"Anxious, I guess," I told him.

"Who wouldn't be?" He looked at the back of Felicia's head. "What about you, princess? You nervous?"

She crossed her arms and looked out the window.

"Sullen," Stan told me.

"You're baiting her," I said. "Leave her alone for a while."

He watched me in the rearview mirror. "What was your wife's name, Elliot? The one you used to have."

I looked at the road ahead of me. "Carrie."

"What did you say happened to her?"

"We got divorced."

"That's right. I don't think you ever told us why. Don't you think Felicia has a right to know why you got divorced? Might tell her something important about her knight in shining armor."

Felicia looked at me.

To Stan I said, "I'm no one's knight in shining armor."

He smiled. "How come I feel like you keep skimping on the story of your life, Elliot?"

I shook my head.

"I don't want to talk about it," I said.

Felicia turned away from me and leaned her head against the passenger's side window and watched the night sky.

Stan watched me in the mirror.

I didn't say anything to him, and we rode in silence. I don't know what Felicia was thinking about. Maybe she was too scared to think. Maybe she was plotting her next move. I'm certain that's what Stan was doing.

I wasn't. I was watching the road slip beneath us. I was thinking about the road slipping away behind me.

I thought about Carrie getting out of that man's car and walking into the hospital to see me. It seemed like a memory from my childhood, or worse, like one of those faint recollections that could be equal parts memory and invention. Maybe I hadn't really seen her at all. Maybe I only thought I had. Either way, it seemed so far away from where I was, driving up Interstate 40 with two strangers and two dead bodies, as to not really matter.

Garbage 12

Stan directed me toward an exit. "Stop at the big gas station," he said. "Pull around back."

I did as he told me, shouldering in front of a church bus full of teenagers and then sliding onto the exit. Just off the service road a fluorescent Exxon station shone like a gaudy beacon in the night. I drove around back.

One light bulb burned over the back door of the gas station. Shadows crowded around the dim circle of light on the door step.

"Park by the door and shut the car off," Stan told me.

Again I did as he said, and we climbed out of the SUV. The parking lot behind the store was tiny. A dozen feet beyond the backdoor, the crumbling pavement simply dissolved into the woods. Stan nodded toward the door. A sign on it read: *Do Not Enter. Employees Only*.

"Push the buzzer there," he said.

Felicia pushed a dirty little button by the doorknob and a minute later, a dumpy, middle-aged man with feathered brown hair opened the door.

"Yes?" he said. He looked past Felicia and me and saw Stan. For a moment, panic darted across his face. "Stan."

"Bruce, need your office."

"My office?"

"Yes. Now."

Bruce looked at Felicia and me. He had the red nose and splotchy pallor of an alcoholic. He bit his sweaty lip and turned back to Stan.

"Sure," he said. "Course, Stan."

Bruce backed out of the way, and we walked through a surprisingly large storeroom and into a rat-hole of an office.

"Go back to work," Stan said over his shoulder, and the middle-aged man turned around without a word and left us.

Stan nodded toward the swivel chair shoved up against the cluttered desk and said, "Felicia."

She sat down and asked, "What are we doing here?"

"You and I are going to call on Fuller while Elliot takes the car down the road."

"What do you mean?" I asked.

"Three miles south down Melnyk Road there's a garbage dump called Thickroot Landfill. Follow the signs to the main building. The place is run by a guy named Arnold Thickroot. Tell him you're there for me."

"And then what?"

"Then he'll dispose of the dearly departed. You'll come back here, and we'll take it from there."

"Why aren't you coming with me?"

"I don't like doing bidness face to face with people I don't have to."

"Can she come with me?"

"No."

I looked back at him. "Why not?"

"Because I need her to meet face to face with Fuller."

"I know Fuller," she told me grimly. "I sort of set this whole thing in motion, so it makes sense for me to do this part."

I asked Stan, "You sure I can handle this, with the ... twins?"

"Yes," he said. "You're smart. You've done well all day today. This part is easy. Short drive. No cops out here. Three miles south down Melnyk Road. Thickroot Landfill. Signs to the main building. Arnold Thickroot. Tell him you're from Stan."

"You'll be here, in the back of this gas station?"

"I've arranged for Felicia to be picked up here by one of Fuller's guys. She'll be brought back here. You meet us back here and we all go back to the truck together."

None of it felt right. I told Felicia, "I hate to leave you."

"This part requires trust," she said. "We've built up trust today, I think."

I wanted to hug or kiss her. I patted her shoulder.

When I walked to the door, Stan said, "Elliot."

I turned around.

"Be smart."

* * *

I pulled out of the parking lot and drove south. It was hilly country out there. Melnyk Road swooped and rose like a roller coaster, while in the distance a jumble of farmland and farmhouses flickered by in the moonlight. After a while, the country closed in, the horse pastures giving way to a narrow corridor of trees. I drove down a steep hill, around a bend, and passed into another land, this one occupied by smaller houses, churches and the occasional gas station.

Dread boiled in my stomach. I tried to think about things, but it was hard to think, alone with two corpses shoved into the backseat.

Still, I tried. I couldn't figure Stan. Why had he come along with me only to bail out at the gas station? Was it as simple as he said or was it something else?

I checked my rearview mirror.

What if I was being set up?

Maybe there was no garbage dump. He could have called and tipped off the cops. I'd be driving around these back roads with two dead bodies, looking for a place that didn't exist.

I passed some houses, a car wash, a Baptist church with a sign out front that read: WHAT PURPOSE IS DRIVING YOUR LIFE?

I checked my rearview mirror. Nothing. I passed more houses, one with a muddy nativity scene still sitting in the yard.

Suddenly a car raced over the hill behind me. It charged up fast. I checked my speed. I was doing the speed limit, thirty-five. The car speeding up my ass was clocking sixty, at least. Its headlights blasted into my rearview mirror, and the car hovered a few feet off my bumper. I waited for the blue lights.

They didn't come. Instead, the car peeked out from behind me so it could see down the black two-lane. Deciding the coast was clear, it passed me. A Honda Civic full of teenagers. One kid flipped me off as they passed, and they all laughed. Once they were in front of me, the driver hit the gas again and they were gone.

I was so busy watching the kids I nearly missed the gravel road jutting out of the woods and the good-sized sign at the end of it reading: THICKROOT.

I slammed on the breaks and the SUV skidded fifty feet, screaming like a soul in hell. When it jerked to a stop, the bodies in the back thumped together.

I shook my head a few times, put the Armada in reverse and backed down the two-lane until I got to the groove-worn gravel road winding off into darkness. I didn't know how far a drive I had, so I eased along, keeping the SUV's wheels in the ruts. I hit the high beams and they jumped out as far as they could, but there was nothing to see except gray trees against a wall of black.

The road snaked off through the trees, and I followed, zigzagging through the darkness like a mouse squirming through a maze. It seemed to go on forever. After a while, I noticed the path ever so slightly easing downward. I picked up some speed. I wanted to get this over with. Then the road steepened, dust swirling in my headlights, gravel snapping under my tires. I followed a sudden, sharp turn, and it spat me out into Thickroot Landfill.

A skinny road subdivided a stinking ocean of trash, then climbed halfway up a distant hill toward a metal shack. A sign along the road read: QUAD 1 SECT 1. I followed the road up the hill and passed sections two, three, four. After a small break between sections, I passed sections five through twenty-five.

Each section was an acre-wide pit, and every inch of that pit stunk like the inside of a septic tank. I had the windows rolled up, but it didn't matter. I didn't try to fight it, either. The putrescence had been there before I showed up, and it would be there a long time after I was gone.

I pulled up to the darkened shack and shone my lights on it. Leaving the SUV running, I got out and peered through a good-sized window next to a wide metal door. With the high beams behind me, I could see a desk, some chairs, a coffee machine, a television. On the wall behind the desk hung a poster of a spotted owl taking a dump on the Constitution over the inscription: EPA: ENVIRONMENTAL PROTECTION ASSHOLES. Another poster featured the same spotted owl wearing an EPA button and wiping his ass with the American flag. Below him was the inscription: I'm Saving Trees By Recycling This Old Flag.

I turned around and looked up the hill. The road twisted through the trash and disappeared over the ridge.

With a shift in the wind, the sharp stench of the garbage suddenly hit me in a wave. I covered my nose and mouth with an arm and ran to the Armada and climbed inside.

"Damn." I slammed the door, but the stink hung on me like I'd been sprayed with cat piss.

I backed onto the road and followed it up the hill. At the ridge, it jerked hard right into the woods again. I followed it and after a few minutes arrived at the top of another pit. I followed the road down into the pit, passing signs for QUAD 2 SECT 1. I passed alongside the sections in the quadrant until I came to another shack halfway up another hill. The shack was smaller than the first, and a light was on in the window.

I stopped and got out. Beside the shack sat a grimy bulldozer. I walked up to the window of the shack but didn't see anybody inside. It had basically the same set up as the first place but no posters. On the wall behind the desk hung a map of the landfill. Colored tacks peppered the board.

I tried the door, found it locked and decided someone must have simply left the light on.

I climbed back into the Armada, drove up the hill, wound through a curtain of trees, and that's when I hit pay dirt. The road dropped sharply into the third quadrant, but from the top of the ridge, past the foul, sprawling acres of garbage, I could see another ridge in the distance. And at the top of that ridge in the moonlight sat a large dark house, its windows aglow.

I swung down into Quad 3, but it was different from the first two, narrower, darker somehow. It occupied a hollow rather than a valley, a rotting cavity among these rolling foothills of garbage.

It smelled worse, too. The stench seemed to claw at the windows as I sped through the acres of trash. Ahead of me in the moonlight, I could see the main road shoot up to the ridge, away from the house.

But at the foot of the hill, next to a crooked sign reading: ThIcKrOoT, a spindly dirt drive crept off from the main road and twisted up toward the house. I wound up the pocked little path, easing over gaping holes and exposed rock, and finally parked beside a dented orange van in the yard.

The house had never been much to look at, I'm sure. Essentially a two-story wooden box with warping gray boards, it clung now to a bald spot on the side of this scrubby hill, its yellowing windows staring out at the swamp of garbage rotting at the edge of the yard.

I got out and slammed my door to announce myself in case whoever was inside had not heard me come up the road.

There was no sign of movement inside the house. I began to walk toward it when somewhere behind me someone said, "Hold it there, asshole."

The Thickroots 13

I stopped and the man behind me said, "Just stand there." Then he called to the house, "All right! I got him!"

The front door of the house opened and spilled light into the dirt yard. A round man clutching a shotgun stepped outside.

With the light at his back, I had a hard time seeing his face. Tufts of black hair stuck out above his ears, but his head was as bare as the moon. He wore jagged old spectacles held together by clumps of duct tape.

"Who are you?" he asked in a dirty baritone.

"Stan the Man sent me."

"Who?"

I blinked.

He stepped to the left, and the house's illumination hit me like a floodlight. After a moment, though, when my eyes adjusted, I could see him a little better. Fleshy cheeks bunched around a greasy ball of a nose. Heavy, stupid eyes peered at me behind the spectacles.

"Well?" he said.

"I'm looking for Arnold Thickroot," I said. "Stan the Man told me to deliver a package," I jerked my head toward the SUV, "to Arnold Thickroot."

"That a fact?"

"Yes, it is."

He glanced at the name badge on my shirt. "Your name Juan?"

"Sure."

"Kinda pale for a Juan."

"My mother was an albino."

He laughed and scratched the two days worth of stubble on his chin. "All right, Juan. I'm Thickroot."

"Then I have a package for you, Mr. Thickroot."

The fat man lowered his gun. "Well, I guess I better see what you got." To the man in the darkness behind me, he said, "Three, you keep an eye on him."

"All right," Three answered. I didn't turn to look for him, but his thin voice sounded young.

Thickroot gestured to the Armada. I turned and walked to the back and lifted the hatch. The two packages lay stiffening in their cramped casket, and at some point— perhaps when I'd hit the brakes back on the two-lane—one of them had popped open, and part of a face peered out. I couldn't tell who it was. Ashen-skinned, his rolled-back eye turning a milky gray, he'd lost any hold to identity.

"Well," Thickroot said, "he's dead as all hell."

I nodded. "Yes, he is."

He covered the dead man's face. "You do that?"

"No."

"Stan?"

I shrugged.

Thickroot nodded and called out, "All right, Three. C'mon out of there."

The man who stepped out of the dark holding a shotgun turned out to be a dirty, chop-haired girl. She couldn't have been a day over seventeen, but she looked me in the eye with a steadiness Thickroot lacked. Broad-shouldered and heavy-set like her father, she was about as delicate as a brick. She wore jeans and, despite the heat, a dark flannel shirt. Near her heavy work boots hovered an old dog, dirty, mangy and pregnant.

The girl looked me over.

"Hi," I said.

To her father she said, "You want me to get the truck?"

"Yeah. And the dozer. Get it all ready."

"Where you want to take 'em?"

Thickroot frowned at the girl. "Where do you think?"

"Sixteen?"

"Course. Move your ass."

The girl stepped toward her father, the gun pointed at the ground. "Don't try to show off, Arnold."

Neither father nor daughter backed down until, at the same time, they both seemed to step away. Thickroot cradled his gun in the crook of his left arm. The girl wandered back into the dark trailed by the silent dog.

Thickroot shook his head, and said, "She'll probably be a little while. You come on in the house with me."

I turned to see where the girl was, but she and the dog were gone.

Thickroot said, "My girl, Arnold Thickroot the third. I just call her Three."

"Was she just hanging around out here? Waiting for somebody to drive up?"

Thickroot didn't answer as he turned and walked back toward his house.

I followed him up to the house. He walked inside and left it to me to close the door. A small foyer led into a wide, bright den with high cream-colored walls and a large ceiling fan. An enormous burgundy recliner, which looked to be of a set with an enormous burgundy sofa, sat in front of an enormous flat-screen television against the wall. And on the television was a porn movie. On the single bookcase against the wall sat rows of porn DVDs and tapes. The house looked like it had been decorated by a middle-class suburban sex addict.

Thickroot walked through the room without glancing at the people—four of them if I counted right—fucking on the TV screen. He disappeared into the kitchen.

I stared at the orgy for a minute. The sound was turned down, and the bodies onscreen copulated with silent vigor.

"Hey man, you care for a drink?" Thickroot called from the kitchen.

As if he had flipped a switch in me, I suddenly realized I was starving. I couldn't remember the last time I had eaten. I hurried after him into the kitchen and found him standing in front of the refrigerator, the gun still tucked into his armpit. Dishes filled the sink, but not in a gross way. They were dishes from tonight's dinner, not last week's. Likewise, the kitchen—and what I'd seen of the rest of the house— seemed to be clean and furnished by Target and Bed, Bath & Beyond. An island anchored the middle of the room and the wide windows looking out onto an empty backyard seemed to expand it.

"I'm starving," I said. "And I haven't had anything to drink for a while."

Thickroot turned and looked me up and down. "I got some leftover mac and cheese," he said.

"That sounds delicious."

He pulled out some blue Tupperware and held it out to me. "Microwave's broke," he said.

I told him thanks, said I loved cold macaroni and took the tub to the island. He handed me a fork.

"What you want to drink?" he asked.

I shook my head. I was already forking down clumps of the macaroni as fast as I could.

He handed me a Budweiser and a Fresca. "Either one or both. Help yourself." He leaned against the counter and watched me eat.

I cracked open the can of soda and swallowed some.

"You are hungry," he said.

"Yeah," I said.

He nodded. "Sorry there ain't nothing but old mac and cheese. The girl ain't much of a cook, I reckon. She's okay, though. Keeps me fat, anyway."

I waved that away. When I stopped to breathe for a moment, I told him, "This is the greatest meal of my life."

Thickroot laughed. "Then you're worse off than me, and that's saying something."

I nodded. "You don't know the half of it."

"Aw hell, man, I bet Stan pays pretty well."

Having nothing to say about that, I kept eating.

He asked, "So how'd you come to be working for Stan?"

I stopped shoveling down macaroni. Everything about the situation told me not to trust Thickroot. I had a sip of the soda and told him, "Just lucky, I guess."

"That Stan, he's a funny one," Thickroot said.

"Yeah."

"Why'd he kill them two out there?"

It occurred to me Thickroot probably didn't know DB was a cop.

"I don't really know," I said. "I mean, it happened so fast. I wasn't expecting it and then …" I just let the sentence wander off. Then I had some more macaroni.

Thickroot shrugged. "Well, Stan's one crazy son of a bitch of a man. No figuring a crazy bastard like that."

I finished the macaroni, washed it down with the soda and cracked open the can of beer. I took a long pull off it.

Thickroot laughed at my face. "You've had a rough day. I can tell."

I kissed the side of the can. "Liquid gold."

"How long did you say you been working for Stan?"

"I don't work for him."

"Really?" Thickroot jerked his bald knob of a head toward the yard. "You're driving around a couple of dead guys for him. If you ain't working for him, you must be one hell of a friend."

I took a long slow drink and said, "I owe him."

"Money?"

"A favor."

Thickroot lifted his heavy eyebrows and said, "Well, it's a tough thing, being indebted to a fella like Stan, I reckon." Something had changed in his face, though. He'd lost all interest in me. He pulled a beer out of the fridge, and I followed him into the den. Still standing, I watched him settle down into the big recliner. He propped the shotgun against the recliner's arm. Then he pushed out the footrest, folded his arms on his gut like a drunk might relax on a bar, and stared at the television.

The movie had moved into something resembling a plot. A blonde with enormous breasts was sitting at a desk talking to a ponytailed man in a business suit.

After a while, they started kissing. They were peeling off each other's clothes when I heard a truck pull into the driveway. A minute later the girl walked in the front door. She held it open just long enough for the dog to walk in, then she slammed it shut. Thickroot jerked around in his recliner.

"You ready?"

"Yeah," the girl said. She stood there by the door and acted as if I wasn't there. She could only have been sixteen or seventeen, but I could tell that her years were the equal of most people's lives. The old dog sat down next to her, its dirty, swollen belly plump against the floor. They both smelled like they'd been wading in a sewer.

Thickroot turned to me and put on some of the friendliness he'd had in the kitchen. "How about you, Elliot? You ready? We'll get your packages all stowed and taken care of and you can get on out of here."

"Sure," I said.

He smiled. Friendly.

I nodded. I even gave a curt smile back. But Thickroot had used my name. And I hadn't told him my name.

Audrey 14

Thickroot stood and picked up his gun. He jerked his head toward the back of the house, and the girl followed him. The dog followed the girl. "We'll be just a minute," he told me.

I shook my head. *Think, damn it. He knows your name. What does that mean? You didn't say it, right? You made a crack about your name being Juan.*

What are they in there talking about?

You didn't use your name did you?

Stan could have called him and told him you were coming. But why did Thickroot give you the third degree when you showed up? Was he just being careful? Or—

When Thickroot & Daughter walked back into the room something had changed between them. The girl ducked her head, hands shoved in her pockets, shotgun tucked under her arm, and stalked to the front door. The dog loped after her. At the door, she turned around.

Thickroot carried his shotgun like a caveman clutching a club. He stopped at the doorway of the kitchen and barked at his sullen child. "You just gonna stand there with your thumb up your ass?" he asked.

The dog barked back at him.

The girl glanced at me. Then she turned, opened the door and stomped outside, the dog following.

"Goddamn cunt," Thickroot muttered. He jerked his head at the door and told me, "Sorry about that, man. She's stubborn. But we got you all set up. Let's go." Before he started for the door, he glanced back at the television screen. After a brief interlude of plot, the porn had gone back to a sex scene.

I stood up. My nerves jangled with indecision. He waited for me. I walked past him.

Outside, he told me, "Three's going to ride with you. I'll follow."

The girl stood by the driver's side of the Armada and waited.

"Really?" I said.

Thickroot shrugged that off. "She's an old pro at this. Been doing it since she was a kid."

I looked back at the girl. Her short brown hair drew to a point on her forehead, just above her pissed-off expression. I suppose if I'd been bulldozing garbage and corpses all my life, I'd be pissed off, too.

"Sure," I told Thickroot.

Thickroot stared at me for a moment.

I asked, "Is there anything else?"

"Nope," he said.

I put my hand out to shake. A weird smile twisted onto his face, and he put his meaty paw out. We shook, and I walked down to the Armada.

"Make more sense to let me drive it," the girl said. She had a low voice for a girl.

"Sure," I said. I threw her the keys, and she caught them with one hand. I walked around to the passenger side and got in while she opened the back door for the dog. Panting, the dog struggled into the backseat.

The girl climbed in the driver's seat and fired up the SUV. She backed out, and I watched her father watch us. He stood there a moment, scratched his gut, and carried his shotgun down to the orange van.

Three tore off into the woods. After only a minute, I couldn't tell if we were still on a road. I didn't see Thickroot following us.

The kid and the dog both stunk like all hell. I thought about rolling down the window, but there was no point. It smelled worse outside.

The girl sat up close to the wheel. Sweat beaded her forehead and chin.

After a moment of silence, the dog shoved her head between our seats. I rubbed behind her ears. "What's your dog's name?"

The girl sucked in her lower lip. "Audrey," she answered finally. "Arnold thinks her name is Bitch. That's what he calls her; the name he give her. But her real name's Audrey. That's the name I give her."

"Audrey's better than Bitch, I'd have to say."

The girl lit a cigarette and the vehicle soon filled with smoke. It was an improvement on the smell. "She's a good dog," the girl said. "Follows my ass everywhere, like that little blue dog in the Dagwood cartoons."

"Daisy."

"Yeah. Like Daisy." She stuck the cigarette in her mouth and let it dangle while she rubbed the dog's dirty little head.

In a soft voice, she said, "Old Audrey's gonna have puppies pretty soon."

I nodded. We bounced over a hill and reconnected to something resembling a path.

"Where we're going's pretty far out," Three explained. "Obvious reasons for that."

"Sure," I said.

The third quad differed from the first two. When I'd driven through the first two parts of the landfill, everything lay spread out in a grid, with sections of trash on each side. This third part, however, was a contorted piece of country. The hollows dug deeper and a dark river of trash coursed down into them. We followed the path of this river until we seemed to be driving down into the trash; it rose above us on either side, hills of it. Soon the natural landscape surrendered, and I saw the last of the treetops clawing at the night sky before we descended completely into the canyon of garbage. Fat trash bags, stray bottles, diapers, wrappers, rotting food, shattered glass, fragments of furniture—all of it stacked seventy, eighty, ninety feet high. The mounds of sludge and waste dipped and rose like the curving of a mountain range.

Our path narrowed and twisted like a single kinky strand of fabric, and Three slowed down. I checked behind us, but I didn't see Thickroot.

"Your dad must be far back there."

She took the cigarette out of her mouth. "Yeah. Must be."

"I notice you call him Arnold."

The girl took a final drag from her cigarette, lowered the power window, and flicked it into the wind. "It's his name."

"And yours."

"I didn't ask for it."

"No one ever does. You're the third. Did you know your grandpa?"

"Yeah," she said. "He was a good one, I guess, but he didn't know what the hell was going on most of the time." Her eyes glanced at me and then went back to the road. "But who does?"

"Yeah. Do you get along with your father?"

"You talk a lot," the girl said, not impatiently but as a statement of fact.

"I guess. I used to be a preacher. Got paid to talk."

"No kidding, a preacher?"

"Yeah."

"I never knew a preacher before. What's a preacher do besides talk on Sunday?"

"Visit people. Old folks, families with problems. I did a lot of work with troubled youth."

She pressed closer against the steering wheel, her thick arms hugging it close. "I'm a youth with troubles."

I looked down at my hands. "I know."

"How do you know?"

"Well," I said. "I mean, doing this kind of thing." I motioned to the back of the SUV. It seemed like the bodies were starting to stink, but I couldn't tell. The whole damn world stunk at that point.

"What kind of thing?"

"Dumping bodies," I said. "I imagine it must bother you."

The girl dug out another cigarette from the pack in her shirt pocket. She lit it and said, "It don't bother me. I done worse."

The macho bluster. I'd seen it in Stan, seen it in DB, seen in a hundred pimply faces over the years. Hell, I'd seen it in myself. And what was it? Nothing but a magic trick, a sleight of hand: Watch this hand, and my pain and fear just disappear. Magic. Thickroot had raised Three to be a fucked-up boy, and, in some ways, that's exactly what she reminded me of.

"It would bother me," I said.

The girl chuckled. "I don't know why," she said. She wagged her thumb over her shoulder. "You brung these ones here with you."

"They're not mine."

Three laughed at that.

"Tell it to the cops," she said.

"I guess you have a point," I said. "Still, I don't know what kind of—and, I don't mean anything by this, but I just … I don't know what kind of man makes his daughter do this kind of thing. Makes me feel bad to be here."

Three said, "Well, Arnold's a piece of shit. Thing I can't figure is how Old Number One produced such a son. That don't hardly make sense. Old Number One wasn't perfect, mind you. He ruint hisself on booze till he finally drunk hisself into the ground. But he was always more harm to hisself than anybody else. Arnold, though. He's meaner'n a dump rat."

"I'm sorry to hear that."

The girl stared at the road, but even from the side I could tell she had something in her eyes which her father simply lacked. She might be poorly educated and ill-raised, but she had a natural thoughtfulness. "What would you a-told me when you was a preacher? I mean, if I had come to you and said what I just said?"

"I would have offered to help you."

Hugging the wheel, she sucked on her lip and watched the headlights claw the corridor of trash.

I said, "I can offer to help you now."

"How?"

"You don't have to stay here. You can leave. I could help you leave."

"Sure you could. I bet you're real fucking touched by my predicament."

"I've dealt with lots of kids with bad parents. More than you know. I know it's tough, but it's not a destiny. You can still be your own person."

"You're right about that. You think I want to stay in this shithole my whole life?"

"No, I don't."

She leaned back a bit and shot me an incredulous look. "How are you going to come in here and offer to help me? You don't even know me, man."

"You know what, Three? Nobody knows anybody. It's all guesswork. I look at you and I see a kid raised in a stinking dump with a no-good father. Am I wrong?"

"No, that's pretty spot on."

"All I'm saying is, you still have a choice. He hasn't got that part of you deep down inside of you, that part you've hidden from him, that part you've protected from him. That part is still yours. You can still hold on to it."

She smiled.

"What?" I said.

"You was a preacher, huh?"

I chuckled. "Yeah. I guess my preacher gene flares up every now and then. But I'm serious, Three. If you're in trouble, I do want to help you."

She glanced at me and then back to the path coiling deeper into the trash mounds. "You're the one in trouble."

"What do you mean?"

"Nothing."

"Three, what do you mean?" I looked behind us. Still nothing.

The kid shook her head. "Nothing. I should keep my mouth shut."

"You meant something by that. Where's your father? I don't see his van."

"He's coming." She hugged the steering wheel again. "You don't know what's going on here, do you?"

"Maybe not. Why don't you tell me?"

"What do you think?"

"Well, right now I'm thinking Stan called your father."

"Arnold."

"Arnold. Stan called Arnold. He told him I was coming. Told him who I was. Told him to get rid of me."

The girl slowed down.

"Well?" I said. I looked behind us again.

We crawled to a stop. Garbage towered above us on each side.

Audrey stuck her head between us. Three rubbed her ears.

"That's pretty much the situation," Three said.

"Jesus," I muttered. I looked behind us.

"He ain't back there," the girl said.

"Where is he?"

Still rubbing Audrey's ears, Three jerked her chin ahead of us. "Section sixteen."

"What's supposed to happen there?"

The girl shrugged like I was asking her what had happened at school that day. "We're supposed to get rid of you."

I stared at her.

"We done this sort of thing before," she said. "While you was up at the house with Arnold, I come out here and bulldozed up a hole. We're supposed to shoot you, throw you in the hole, cover it up and then push a bunch of trash on top."

I thought about the way Thickroot had sized me up back at the house. He had been sniffing around to see if there was some extra money. When I'd made it clear I was just running errands for Stan, he'd decided to just go ahead and kill me.

"Now what, Three?"

She opened her door, cradled her shotgun and stepped out. "C'mon, Audrey," she said gently. The dog climbed onto the driver's seat, and the girl scooped her up and set her on the ground. She pointed down the road and told me, "Keep going right. It'll lead you back to the main road."

I climbed over to the driver's seat.

"Wait," I said. "Felicia …"

"What?"

"Do you know what Stan was going to do with Felicia?"

"I don't know," the girl muttered. "I don't know nothing about nobody named Felicia. Arnold didn't mention nothing about a woman."

"Why are you helping me?" I asked.

The girl squinted down the path ahead of her. "'Cause you're the only one ever offered to help me," she said. She turned and spit into the trash. "But you can't help me, though. It's blood on blood, this thing between me and him. It's been coming at me my whole life. I always knowed it, too. I guess it's gotta come to a head tonight. I hadn't figured it that way, but I reckon that's the way it's shaking out." Audrey nuzzled her leg, and Three scratched her head.

I stared at her. "Thanks," I said finally.

She thought about that, rubbed the dog's head some more, and shrugged.

* * *

I had no idea where the hell I was, had no idea what contortions the path would take, but I sped away as quickly as I could.

I didn't get far before I had to stop.

I sat there and thought—or tried to think anyway.

As a couple of huge rats scurried through the headlights, something gnawed at me. I wanted to get out of this shitty hole in the earth as soon as I could. I had to get back to Felicia.

Either she was with Stan in setting me up or she was in worse trouble than me. Either way made sense, if you looked at it objectively. She might be with him. She might have been with him from the start. Maybe I'd been brought in at the last moment to be a fall guy. That would make sense.

But the other way was possible, too. Stan had murdered two people, one of whom was a police officer. Now, he'd tried to eliminate me as a witness. He could easily do the same to Felicia—maybe have this Fuller guy kill her. If so, I had to move fast if I was going to protect her.

But I sat there with the SUV idling.

Looking back over my shoulder, back down that dark path twisting through the mountains of trash, I couldn't see anything. I thought of that girl on her way to a confrontation with her father.

I dropped the phone and ran. Out my office door, down the hall, down the steps. Tree limbs bent in the wind and leaves slapped at a sky drained of color. My car was parked in my usual space.

I jerked the wheel to the right, pulled up until the grill kissed the trash mounds, then I backed up. After a couple of tries, I'd turned around completely.

I headed back toward Section 16, back toward Three and Audrey and Arnold Thickroot Jr.

Section 16 15

I heard them before I saw them. I'd parked beside a tin marker with the number 16 on it and climbed out of the SUV, starting down the path on foot, figuring it must lead to a clearing of some kind. A thin wisp of cloud drifted across the moon like cigarette smoke and gave everything below a milky-blue tint. I fumbled along as quietly as I could, looking at the trash pile for a weapon of some kind but all I found was an old-fashioned Coke glass bottle with the heavy bottom. I clutched the neck of the bottle like a billy club and crept down the path not knowing quite what I would do when I got there. I didn't know what Three had planned, but I didn't want to leave her to it alone. That much I was decided upon.

I hadn't gone far when I heard Thickroot's voice. I couldn't make out what he was saying, but it sounded indignant. I hurried closer, and as I rounded the mound of garbage I saw the light from his truck pointing away from me.

After the turn around the trash pile, the road I was on dropped so sharply that I was looking down on them.

Thickroot's truck, sitting beside a bulldozer, pointed at a hole in the dirt a few yards ahead, its high beams shining down into what was supposed to be my grave.

Thickroot, clutching his shotgun, stood beside his truck. His daughter stood further away, mostly obscured in the darkness with Audrey somewhere behind her.

Thickroot slapped the hood of his truck.

"You're a fucking sight to see," he told his daughter. "You're a fucking sight to see. Walking up here with that mangy dog and a stupid ass look on your face."

The girl said something I didn't hear.

Thickroot waved it away.

The girl said something else, and Thickroot causally pointed his shotgun at the sky and fired once. At the boom I jumped and dropped my bottle, but neither of them heard me. I picked up the bottle as the echo of Thickroot's shotgun whispered past me.

I moved closer to them in the dark.

"What am I supposed to tell Stan?" Thickroot asked his daughter.

As I got closer, I could begin to make out Three in the moonlight. She stood with her weight on one leg, the shotgun tucked under her arm.

She said, "Tell him the guy never showed up."

Thickroot rubbed his chin. "I could tell him that."

"Or," the girl said, "tell him you don't want to kill people and bury bodies no more."

"Just like that?"

"Just like that."

Thickroot spat in the dirt. "You're so tough, why don't you fucking tell him?" He spat again. "Little cocksucker.

Maybe I should let you explain to him why you let the fucking guy go."

"I'll tell him," the girl said.

"I know," his father scoffed. "You got such balls now. You want to talk to him, you go right ahead."

I stopped at the bottom of the hill and crouched behind some fat plastic trash bags with damp, shredded paper sticking out the ends like soppy white tongues.

"I can't hardly believe you're my father," the girl said.

"Well, that makes two of us," Thickroot said.

Three nodded. "I reckon." Audrey stood beside her staring at Thickroot with contempt.

The father said, "You just let him go?"

"Yep," his daughter answered.

"Just like that? You just let him go?"

The girl didn't answer. She didn't like to waste words. She'd said what she'd said, and she didn't see any use repeating it.

Her father slapped the hood of the truck again, walked to the edge of the grave and kicked a plastic cup into it. Slowly, he turned around and looked at his daughter.

"He give you some money or something?"

"No."

"You sure he didn't give you no money?"

"What put that idea in your head?"

"Cause at least that would make some goddamn sense."

"Not to me it wouldn't."

"You sure you ain't got a pocket full of cash right now?"

"I ain't got a nickel."

"How about I search you and we find out?"

"You ain't putting your hands on me," Three said. She held the shotgun at her side now. "I done told you that a long time ago."

"You threatening me?" her father said.

"I'm telling you the way it is," Three said. "You lay a hand on me, and I'll kill you."

"Your own daddy?" Thickroot asked, almost amused.

"I'll blow your damn head off and throw you in that ditch right there. And you know I'll do it, too."

"Your own daddy," Thickroot said wistfully. "Sad state of affairs."

"Just so we're straight on things."

"Sure," her father said. "We're straight. I just want to know what we're gonna do when Stan comes around."

"We'll deal with it," Three said.

"Yeah. I guess." Thickroot nodded at the truck, "C'mon, let's go up to the house and figure out how the fuck we're gonna deal with this mess."

The girl said okay and whistled at Audrey. They walked toward the truck, but when the girl walked past her father to the passenger side, Thickroot struck her face with the butt of his gun. The girl fell, and the dog yelped.

Thickroot kicked his daughter in the stomach.

"Who the fuck do you think you are?" he yelled.

The dog barked at him, and Thickroot kicked her in the stomach again. Then he spun around and kicked away her shotgun.

He spun back toward her. "You want to threaten me, you little cocksucker?" He kicked the girl in the head. "You want to threaten me!"

He kicked her in the chest, and I ran from behind my hiding place. I knew I had one chance. I was too far away to run at him and hope not to get shot, but I was close enough to make a throw at his head with the bottle. I ran as close to him as I dared and hurled the bottle at his head.

It hit him like a rock. The bottle didn't even break, and Thickroot staggered backward. For an instant, I thought he would regain his footing, but then his right foot stepped on his left foot, and he tumbled to the ground. The girl struggled up and made a wobbly run for her gun. Thickroot, shaking his head and trying to get to his feet, fired at her but had a better chance of hitting the moon. He didn't know what the hell was going on. He fired at Three again, but the girl was in the darkness, and the kick of the shotgun knocked Thickroot back.

Summoning my voice, I yelled, "Hey!"

Thickroot spun around in the mud toward me. As I jumped into the darkness, a shotgun fired.

I crouched in a runner's starting pose behind the remains of a rotted sofa, ready to make a run up the hill, zigzagging in the dark.

Then I noticed silence. I turned back around and ventured a peek around the sofa and saw the girl standing over her father. The dog stood beside her. They were both staring down at the hole in Arnold Thickroot's chest.

"Hey," I yelled.

The dog looked over at me. Then she looked up at the girl. Three kept staring at her father.

"Yeah," Three finally answered.

"I'm coming out," I said. I stood up and walked across the soggy, stinking earth toward her.

When I got to her, she nodded down at her old man. Thickroot clutched his gun, his eyes open wide. Beneath his broken glasses his temple was still bleeding from where I hit him with the bottle, but the red hole smoking in the middle of his chest left no doubt he was dead.

"I come at him from under the truck," the girl said. "When he turned to get you, I shot him in the back."

"Are you okay?" I asked.

The girl shook her head. "He's dead. Died a couple seconds ago, when you was walking over here from your hiding spot."

"I'm sorry."

The girl rubbed the bruise already starting to swell on her cheek, then looked up at me. "You hit him with a rock or something?"

"A Coke bottle."

She pointed at her father with the shotgun, its barrel still smoking a little. "You hit him with a Coke bottle."

"Yes."

She stared down at her dead father. She rubbed her cheek and winced as she did it. She seemed to be avoiding looking at me.

"Guess you had to do it," she said finally. "Guess you didn't have much of a choice, him kicking me and all."

I grasped for something to say. "I'm sorry about your father, Three."

She raised her head, her eyes empty and hard. "I told you. His name is Arnold."

"Right. Arnold."

"He never was a father. Old Number One raised me 'cause Arnold was too worthless. When Old Number One died, I was on my own. Arnold was more like a boss. A mean one."

"I see."

We both regarded the dead man at our feet.

"I was trying to help you," I offered. "I came back to help you. I didn't want to leave you here to face him alone. Him and maybe Stan."

The girl wiped sweat from her face with the back of her grimy hand. "Stan," she said. "I forgot about him for a minute."

I wanted to reach out and touch her shoulder, but I couldn't, and I knew she wouldn't want me to, anyway.

"Are you okay?" I asked.

"You asked me that already," the girl said. "You think I got any better in the last three minutes?"

"No," I said. "You're right. I'm sorry."

The girl stared at Arnold some more. "I should bury him."

I looked down at him.

She asked, "You think that's a good idea?"

"I don't know."

"You want to call the cops?"

I thought of Felicia and Stan. I thought of the dead cop and his brother in the back of the SUV I'd been driving around.

"That's not … it's not what I would want."

"No, me neither."

I nodded.

"Okay then," she said.

"I'll help you."

"Grab his legs."

Three leaned her gun against the truck. Then she pried her father's gun out of his hand and leaned it against the truck, too. I picked up the man's feet, clutching his thick ankles through dirty socks. Three grabbed his arms. We took a few steps when the arms began to slide, and Three dropped her father, lurched away a few steps, and fell to her knees.

I watched her for a moment, then I dragged Arnold Thickroot to his grave and shoved him in. He slid down, pushing a wave of mud in front of him. When he stopped, he lay hunched over, a muddy, bloody black hole between his shoulder blades.

I walked over to the girl. "I'm going to bring down the car and throw the other two in here with …"

Three nodded.

I walked, then ran, to the SUV. When I drove back to the grave, the girl was standing at the truck, staring at her father. I backed up to the pit and got out. Without saying anything to her, I opened the back and hauled out the first twin. The body hit the damp ground, but the kid didn't move. I dragged the body to the pit and pushed it in. It slid down, half lying on Thickroot.

The girl took a deep breath, walked to the SUV, pulled down the other body and pushed it in the grave. She did it all with a minimum of movement, with no look on her face except a concentration of effort to get the job done.

"Need to quicklime them," she said walking toward her father's truck. When she came back, she carried a white plastic bucket. She pried the lid off, pulled out a decapitated milk jug full of white powder and shook it over the bodies. Then she scooped out a few more jugfulls and powdered the bodies until they were completely covered.

She took the bucket back to the truck while I stared down at the three dusty bone-white corpses in the pit below me.

A moment later, she walked up beside me.

"What are you thinking?" she asked, looking down at her father and other two dead men.

I didn't say anything, but I gestured at the bodies.

The girl nodded. "I'm pretty sure a jury would say we both killed Arnold. Especially once we bury him and these other two."

"I suspect that's true."

She watched me for a minute, then she asked, "What are you gonna do now?"

I rubbed my face. "I'm not sure. Everything has happened so fast."

"You gonna go up against Stan the Man?"

I looked at the dead men in the hole. "I think I have to."

"He's a pretty bad dude."

"Yeah. I know."

"You ever shot a gun?"

"No."

"Ever been in a fight?"

I shrugged. "Not really."

Three put her hands on her hips and crooked her head. "So why are you gonna take on Stan? That don't make a lot of sense."

"There's a woman."

"A woman."

"Yeah."

The girl pulled out her cigarettes and lit one. She blew out some smoke and said, "You love her?"

I shook my head. "Not exactly," I said.

"Then why do it?"

"I feel like I need to protect her."

"How come?"

"How come you didn't let Arnold kill me?" I asked.

She took a drag off her cigarette, peered at me as she blew out the smoke and said, "Okay. But is it gonna do her any good for you to get your head blowed off?"

"That's not the point."

"What's the point?"

I wiped some mud from my hands. "I killed myself yesterday. I killed myself, and they brought me back in the ER."

The girl stared at me for a while thinking about that. Then she took another pull off of her cigarette and said, "So, what, this is like a second chance or something?"

"No," I said. "But this is a decision to make. And for a long time, I thought I was out of decisions."

"So this is your decision, then, to go up against Stan and try to protect this woman?"

"Yes."

Smoking her cigarette and squinting against the smoke, the girl looked at me long and hard for a while.

"Well, I could sit here at the dump and wait to see what will happen to me or I could go with you."

"No one's asking you to help me."

"I know, but if you run off and get killed I ain't got no reason to think Stan won't come in here and knock me off."

I didn't know how to respond to that. From what I knew of Stan, it was probably true.

Finally, the girl dropped her butt, stubbed it out in the stinking mud and asked, "So do you want some help or not?"

"I wouldn't feel right about it."

She said, "You'd feel alright leaving me here alone? I thought you offered to help me before."

"How would taking you to face Stan be a way of helping you?" I said, but I caught myself. Maybe there was a way to help her.

The money. All that goddamn money.

"For what I've done for Stan," I said, "and for what he's tried to do to me, he owes me."

The girl didn't know what I meant, but she waited on me.

I said, "What would you do with a million dollars?"

Cleaning 16

The girl and I buried her father and the twins under a few tons of trash. Working the bulldozer in a cloud of exhaust fumes, she pushed sludge and filth over her father's grave. The bulldozer roared and spat mud and smoke into the air, but I was acutely aware of the silence beyond our darkened hollow. We sat at the raging center of nothing.

When the girl finished, she drove the bulldozer up the hill. Then she walked back down and drove her father's truck to the house. I followed her in the Armada, watching her thick white arm hang out the driver's side window and Audrey's head hang out the passenger side.

When we got back to the house, she jumped out of the truck and walked over to me. She held up Arnold's cellphone.

"Good," I said. I gestured at our sweaty, muddy clothes and hair. "We should clean up, quickly. We smell like a couple of sewer rats, and we don't want to call any more attention to ourselves than we have to."

The girl nodded but didn't move.

"It's all right if you're having second thoughts," I said. "I understand."

"It ain't that," she said. "I want to go with you."

"Then what?"

She put her hands on her hips and jerked her head toward the house. "Fact is, I been wondering how to keep everyone from finding out. People knowed me and Arnold fought like a couple of roosters. They're gonna think I killed him just to be done with him." She thought about that for a second. "And the fact is, I can't say it wouldn't a-happened that way eventually."

"How long will it take people to miss him?"

The girl shrugged. "Arnold didn't have no friends to speak of, but we got people in here all the time dropping off garbage. I reckon I could tell them he run off, but where would Arnold have run off to? That's the question. Folks might get suspicious."

"Are you thinking we shouldn't have buried him?"

"No," the girl said firmly. "I shot him in the back. If we woulda called the police, they woulda tossed us both in jail. Then the police woulda found them other two." She stared at my face a moment. "What?"

"What?" I said back.

"You got a funny look on your face. Who was them other two we buried out there?"

I rubbed my face, but my hand was greasy. My arms felt heavy. "Couple of Stan's guys. One of them was a cop."

That news would have jarred most people, even ones who spent all their time among killers and thieves. Finding out you just buried a police officer in a trash pile is hard to hear.

But the girl simply looked away from me, spit into the dark and said, "Well shit." Audrey stared up at her worriedly. Finally she said, "Let me turn that over in my head. We'll get cleaned up and get on the road."

* * *

I showered in a large and clean upstairs bathroom. Like the rest of the house, it stood in stark contrast to the man who'd owned it. Thickroot might have been a son of a bitch who lived at the top of a trash pile, but he liked his comforts. White tiles covered the wall and floors. I scrubbed my body with a yellow exfoliating brush and scented soap. The filth of the garbage dump graveyard spun down the drain between my feet.

As I hurriedly washed the grime out of my hair, I tried to piece together what had happened. Stan had called Thickroot and told him to kill me. Either before we left the twins' house—maybe when Felicia and I were getting dressed—or after I'd left the gas station.

What did Felicia know? Where was she in all of this? It seemed to me that there were three possibilities.

One, she'd been working with Stan from the beginning. My whole involvement was a setup from the start. Maybe they'd always planned to kill the twins. Looking back on the day's events, it seemed like they'd always been on one side and the twins had been on the other.

Two, she was going along with Stan now that he'd decided to get rid of me. After I rode off to deliver the twins to Thickroot, Stan had told her that I was out of the picture. Maybe she felt bad about that. Maybe not. But she and Stan would have five million dollars to split. That kind of money eases a lot of pain.

Three, she was being held hostage without knowing it. Stan would use her to negotiate the new deal with Fuller and then he'd kill her.

I shut off the water, but the sight of a bruise on the back of my right hand jarred me. Brown and yellow, from where the IV had gone in at the hospital, the bruise covered most of the back of my hand but didn't really hurt. I turned my hands over. My palms were pink, wet and clean. Beneath the creased skin, faint green veins. I closed my hands into tight fists, watched my knuckles bulge and whiten. They were good hands, though I'd never put them to much use. I'd turned pages in books, caressed Carrie, caressed myself, lifted bottles to my lips. I'd killed myself with these hands. I'd sinned with these hands, but maybe now I could do something good with them, something discernibly, unequivocally good with them.

Then I thought, *In this shithole world is there such a thing as unequivocal good?*

I laughed and pulled the curtain back and grabbed a towel and hurriedly dried off.

That was the kind question you used to ask. In your first life. No time now for theology or philosophy. Now is a time for doing.

When I stepped out of the shower, I found some blue jeans and a black T-shirt with a breast pocket Three had left folded by the door. I put them on and stared at myself in the mirror.

I'd never been a man of action. For most of my life, I'd contented myself with studying: studying in school, studying in seminary, and once I'd become a full-time pastor, studying for my weekly sermon. But for the past year, I'd drifted: alcohol and oblivion and a series of part-time jobs.

But in this new life, I had no notion that I was going to live forever—neither in this life nor in some eternal realm with Christ. There was nothing left to study except the machinations of Stan's mind.

If Felicia was alive, I would find her. If she was going to betray me, then I would be betrayed. If Stan was going to kill me, then I would die. But I was going to force them both to reckon with me.

Lucky 17

Three had left me white socks and a pair of heavy work boots. I pulled them on and walked down the hall. The upstairs, like the rest of the house, was bright and clean. One hallway ran the length of the upstairs, with the bathroom on one end and the stairs on the other.

The girl came up the steps. Her short hair was still dripping, and she wore the same outfit I did: blue jeans, work boots and a black T-shirt.

"We look like roadies for Johnny Cash," I told her.

"I reckon."

"These your clothes I'm wearing?"

"Yeah. 'Cept the shoes. Those were Arnold's."

"Good fit. Thanks."

"Sure."

She was developing a black eye where her father had hit her.

"You should put ice on that," I said.

"I did," she said. "You ready to go?"

As we walked downstairs she said, "It seems creepy here, now. I want to get out of here."

I followed her out to her truck and we climbed inside. She stashed the shotguns behind the bench seat, fired up the truck and backed down the path. We were almost to the service road before I thought to ask, "Where's the dog?"

"She needs her rest," the girl answered. "She wanted to come, but she needs her sleep."

I nodded.

The girl lit a cigarette. "What's the plan?"

"First," I said. "I should tell you what all has happened."

"Okay, but where am I going?"

"Get on Melnyk and drive toward the interstate."

While the girl drove and smoked, I told her everything that had happened in the last twenty-four hours. I told her about killing myself, about Felicia and the twins and Stan and the truck. I didn't tell her about Carrie. When I finished, she shook her head.

"What's your best bet on what he's thinking?" she asked.

"I have to proceed like Felicia is still alive and she's helping Stan. I want to believe that she didn't have a part in setting me up, but we'll have to see about that."

The cigarette bobbed in her lips as she said, "I was thinking in the shower."

"About what?"

"There's really millions of dollars involved in this deal?"

"Yes."

"And you think we can get it from Stan?"

"If we can get back to the warehouse and get to that truck first, then yes."

She leaned into the wheel and floored the gas. "Holy fucking shit."

When we got to I-40, the interstate lay black and empty and Three tore onto it and pushed the truck as far as it would go.

She said, "I was thinking in the shower that if I get that money you was talking about, I can get the hell away from here. I could sell the place to one of Arnold's old cronies. A lot of people have problems buried in that trash heap. I bet I could sell the place to one of them with no questions asked and then, with the money I get from that and the money I get from Stan, I could get away. Far away from this place."

A swift, unmistakable guilt expanded in my solar plexus, a sensation like falling unexpectedly. What was it? The fear that she would get hurt? The fear that I would give her a dream that would die in front of her?

Then, worried, she said, "What if the truck ain't there?"

I said, "Then he's probably already gotten to it. If the shipment is gone, then I think we're done. But listen, I was thinking, if that does happen you can still sell the place, right? You can still get away. You don't have to be Arnold Thickroot the third anymore."

"Be a lot easier with that money," she said.

The truck rattled down the interstate at its maximum speed, about ninety miles an hour.

"You thought about where we should meet him after we get the truck? Someplace quiet and out of the way?"

"Yes," I said. "I know a place."

* * *

The grounds of the Arkansas Fence Company sat in the still blue darkness of 3 a.m. Three cut her lights and engine and we coasted up to the edge of the grounds.

We got out, and she handed me her father's shotgun.

"I loaded it while you was in the shower," she whispered. "The safety ain't on, so all you got to do is point it and pull the trigger."

We covered the gravel lot between the road and the warehouse on foot. Along with a pair of eighteen-inch bolt cutters, Three carried her shotgun with the ease and familiarity of a favorite tool. I held my gun carefully and tried not to shoot myself in the foot.

When we got to the warehouse, no one seemed to be around. The big doors were closed and padlocked, but Three handed her gun to me and snipped off the lock with the big cutters. As she pulled open the creaking metal doors echoes clattered off into the night.

"Jesus, that's loud," I said.

The space was darker than outside. But there in the shadows sat the truck.

"That it?" she asked.

"Yeah."

She pulled a small flashlight from her back pocket. I hadn't thought to bring one, but at her young age, Three was already more practical than me. She shone a narrow beam on the back of the truck.

I lifted the latch on the back and raised the door.

"That," I told her, "is what all this mess is about."

The pallets of boxes, shrink wrapped in plastic, glinted dimly against the beam of her flashlight.

"Let's go," I said.

"Where's the key?"

I stared at her.

"Elliot ..."

"Shit."

"For Christ's ..."

"Shit!"

"There's gotta be ..." she shone the flashlight across the warehouse to a small glassed-in office tucked back in the corner. "There's got to be keys."

She ran over to the office and went inside. I stood in the dark and watched the light flicker as she went through drawers.

I was recalibrating our plan when she came back to me jiggling some keys. "One of these should work," she said.

She had five different spare keys, none of which were marked. She got it on the third try and unlocked the door to the truck.

"You're lucky I'm here," she said proudly.

"I know. Believe me, kid, I know."

I turned on the truck and backed it out. We rolled across the parking lot, and I stopped at her truck.

"You want me to drive this big one?" she asked. "You don't seem like a guy would know how to drive an eighteen footer."

"Thanks," I said, "but I've driven my share of U-Hauls and church buses."

"Okay," she said. She handed me her father's phone. "Stan's number is under S. Mine is under 3, like the number not the word."

"Okay."

"I'll follow you."

I waited until she got to her truck and then we pulled out. Heading toward the mountains, I took a deep breath, took out Arnold's cellphone, and called Stan the Man.

A beeping. My breathing.

I thought of the signal bouncing from place to place.

A click.

Stan's voice, unmistakable: "Thickroot."

"No, Stan," I said. "Arnold decided to retire."

His breathing.

I would have sworn I could almost hear him smile. "Elliot …"

"After all we've been through tonight, Stan, I thought we were friends. We talked Jesus and the Apostle Paul. We ripped off trucks and bled bodies. And now, after all that, you tried to have me killed?"

"Perhaps this is a discussion we should have face to face and not over the phone," he said.

"Sure," I said. "First, I want to talk to Felicia."

Without saying anything, Stan put her on.

"Elliot?" Her voice. Was it worried? Or just surprised?

"You okay?"

"Yes. I—"

"That's enough," Stan said. "That was her. Why don't we get off the phone?"

"Where should we meet?"

"How about the place with the stuff?"

"Mm," I said, "I don't think so."

"Why not?"

"Cause the stuff's not there anymore."

"What do you mean?"

"I got the stuff."

"Elliot …"

"Stan, shut up. I have the shit. I want to meet to discuss a switch."

Silence.

"You still there?" I asked.

"Go on."

"I want Felicia. And I want a million dollars of the cash you got from Fuller. You owe me that."

"We never agreed on that."

"Yeah, well, when you tried to have me murdered, I decided to renegotiate the terms of our contract. With the twins out of the picture, you can spare a million."

"Perhaps talking about this on the pho—"

"Do I sound like I give a shit about being heard? Do I sound like I'm long term planning?"

"You sound like you've gotten greedy."

"The cash isn't for me. You bring the money and Felicia."

"Where?"

"You know the town of Quigley, north of Fowler about forty-five minutes?"

"Yes," he said. "It seems like there used to be a church there. About a year or so ago."

"That's the one."

"I recall the preacher burned it to the ground."

"I'll be there. A million dollars and Felicia. Then you get your stuff back."

I hung up.

Something Underneath 18

Quigley was a little town scattered for a few miles along Highway 65 in the foothills of the Ozarks. The speed limit dropped to thirty-five miles an hour inside the city limits, but even going that slow you could blow through town in under five minutes. From the highway, there wasn't much to see. Gas stations, fast food franchises, and car repair shops alternated with an almost systematic exactness, a pattern broken only by the occasional house of worship.

I turned off the highway by the Waffle House—the only place occupied at this hour—and Three trailed me down a skinny side road snaking a path through the trees. About a mile down the road, I pulled the truck behind a defunct wholesale bedding outlet.

After locking up the truck, I climbed in with her. "Okay."

"Question."

"Sure."

"Why stash the truck here?"

I gestured for her to take us out the way we'd come in. As she did, I said, "I watched Stan kill two people in a couple seconds. One of those people was a cop who was maybe six feet away and pointing a gun at him."

"You're saying we're fucked."

"I'm saying it's a good idea to tip the odds as much in our favor as possible. If Stan shows up and the truck isn't with us and he doesn't know where it is, the odds of him killing us on the spot go down. This way he gives us the money and Felicia and we lead him to the truck. It slows the process down. That's my thinking anyway."

I directed her down a tangle of back roads and short cuts that eventually deposited us in front of a chipped and rusted metal sign barely peeking out from an overgrow of weeds:

QUIGLEY FREE-WILL BAPTIST
WHERE JESUS IS STILL LORD

"That's it," I said.

Three crept down the road. Outside, everything was quiet. There was no breeze to speak of, no birds singing nor crickets chirping. Only the heavy rolling crunch of the truck's tires.

After a while, the road gave way to the parking lot of the church. In the bruised blue moonlight, I could make out the black skeleton of the building. It wasn't much except a few charred planks stabbing at the sky, but I could see it clearly.

She pulled the truck into the lot and parked away from the remains of the building. We got out.

I took a breath and walked toward the ruins, clutching my shotgun with both hands. Tufts of grass stuck out of the pavement. All that remained of the above-ground level of the church were scorched and rotted planks, but amid the ashes and dirt and broken glass there gaped a rectangular hole. Even in the dim moonlight, I could see the stairs leading down into the lower level.

I walked past the hole to the side lot where I'd once parked my car every day. Beyond it, dew glistened on old playground equipment.

The girl behind me stayed close.

I turned back to the hole.

Three had a small pocket flashlight. She took it out and stepped toward the hole, but I stopped her.

"Give me," I said.

She handed it to me.

Without saying anything else to her, I turned on the light and walked downstairs.

Rotting swatches of red carpet stood out like open sores on the creaking steps. Some chunks of burned paneling still clung to the walls, but by the time I got to the bottom of the stairs the paneling disappeared completely and gave way to a blackened concrete corridor. The melted remains of a stack of chairs slouched against the wall, and a little further down, scorched baby swings hung like stalactites from the ceiling. As I inched down the corridor, long shadows scratched at the walls, and bits of glass and plaster and wood crunched beneath my boots.

Portions of the ceiling had burned away and mold covered what was left. Humidity dripped from exposed pipes and splashed on my head and hands. Sweat stung my eyes.

I stopped and wiped my face with the back of my flashlight-hand, momentarily throwing the corridor into darkness.

Then I heard breathing.

I dropped to a crouch close to the wall, and the flashlight nearly slipped out of my sweaty fist. I held onto it, though, and threw light onto the single doorway at the end of the corridor.

"Hello," I said.

The breathing stopped.

"Hello," I said again, a little louder.

Help me, someone said.

Sweat still stung my eyes, but I didn't move.

Help me, the voice said again.

"Are you alone?"

Yes, the voice said.

I inched toward it, keeping low to the ground. I stopped at the doorway at the end of the hall. I could not see inside, but I could smell something.

Beneath the stink of burned wood and melted plastic, beneath the pungent rot and mildew, I could smell blood.

Please, the voice said.

I stood up and looked in the room.

The Damnation of Brother Stilling 19

It was a giant. He lay chained down on a makeshift table of an old door and two sawhorses. He wore soot-covered slacks, a filthy dress shirt, and a thick, bloody bandage on his right foot. In a pool of blood beneath the table lay a hatchet and half of his foot.

I threw the light into the corners of the room. It had once been a nursery, and burned cribs still sat against the walls. Other than that, we were alone.

The giant shook as I approached him. He'd been beaten and tortured. Dried blood caked his hair and streaked down his face, but his hazel eyes were open and alert and terrified.

"Reverend," I said.

He closed his eyes and took a deep breath. Yes. He took another breath. Though his voice trembled with pain and fear, it was thick and sonorous, and I could tell in an instant what he must have sounded like as he preached. He spat out some blood and said, I never meant to hurt her.

"No," I said. "But you did."

He wept.

"Shut up," I said.

Do you know how many people I helped?

"Does it matter?"

Only if the teachings of Christ are true. If they are, then I've helped ensure the eternal salvation of men, women, and children. God has used me as an instrument to pull souls out of hell. I've done good in this world. In this world and in the next.

"None of that matters."

No?

"No."

You thought it did. For most of your life, you thought it did.

"I was wrong."

You're mad at God.

"Yes."

You're mad at God for your own sin.

"No. I'm mad at God for not existing. I'm mad at the men of God who made me false promises. They told me I wasn't alone. But I am."

You yourself were a man of God.

"Which is just another way of saying I was a liar, too. I lied to myself. I lied to everyone around me. I told lies in this building every day, promised people a home in an invisible heaven far away. It all seems so ridiculous to me now that it makes me sick."

Perhaps. But what about your sin? How will you redeem what you've done?

"The only redemption is deciding what to do next. The sin is mine. I'll bear it myself."

You can't, he said. It will destroy you.

"It already did."

Creaking on the stairs. I shone the light down the hall, and after a moment the girl appeared, pale and small, at the bottom of the stairs. She clutched her shotgun in front of her.

"What the hell are you doing down here?" she asked.

When I didn't answer, she stepped tentatively into the basement.

The hallway was as dark as a mineshaft, and our only illumination was the tiny flashlight. She crept toward me. Stagnant air boiled around us, and sweat cut scars through the soot that collected on our faces.

"What are you doing down here?" she asked. "Are you talking to yourself?"

"Him," I said.

"What?"

I turned.

No one.

The girl watched me. "Why are you down here?"

"This used to be mine," I said.

"Your church?"

"Yes."

"Who burned it down? Muslims?"

"I burned it down."

She stepped closer in the dark to try to see me more clearly. "You?"

"Yes. About this time last year."

"Musta been awful pissed to burn down a church."

"I was mad at God. You can't get angrier than that."

"Why was you so angry?"

I turned away from her and shone the light across the ruins of my church. "I used to tell people in this building every week that believing in God is believing in his promises. The promise that Christ was who he said he was. The promise of eternal life. The promise of protection and guidance. '*Though I walk through the valley of shadow of death I shall fear no evil.*' That kind of thing. I believed it, too. With all my heart. I lived those promises.

"Any why not? I was blessed. I had a wife who loved me. The only woman that I ever loved. We met in college, and we just clicked right away. We got married and went to seminary and roughed it the first couple of hard years. Then God led us here. My first full-time pastorate. The first time I walked in this building I almost cried. Maybe this is just a little podunk town in the middle of nowhere, but I thought God had put me here for a purpose. The promises, you see. Then we had our baby. We'd been trying for a while and then we came here and got pregnant almost right away. The promises.

"Then came August 4th, 2007. We woke up late. We rushed through breakfast and Carrie ran off to work. I loaded up the baby to take her over to Carrie's mother's house. Usually Carrie took her. Then I came to work. I was here half the day. Ate lunch at my desk. I was sitting here writing a sermon when the phone rang. Carrie. Asking me why I hadn't dropped the baby off.

"I ran down the hall. Down the stairs and outside. To the parking lot. To my car. Right where I left it. Where I parked it every day."

The flashlight dropped to the ground.

The girl picked it up. She turned it off.

"Your baby …"

The ash smell filled my nose. I inhaled it deeply.

"I'd forgotten her. She'd gone to sleep in her car seat behind me. I parked, collected my briefcase and my lunch from the passenger seat and walked into work. I sat here in the house of God doing the Lord's work while my daughter died in the parking lot."

The girl didn't know what to say. No one ever did.

She tried.

"It wasn't your fault."

"Yes, it was." More ash, more charred wood and mildew. My eyes stung. "It's an inexplicable lapse. Not of judgment, because I never would have done it on purpose, but a lapse of ... mind. The only thing I know to compare it to is when you drive somewhere, and you're thinking about something else, and when you get to where you're going you realize you have no memory of the drive. The auto-pilot part of your brain did the driving while the active part of your brain planned your day. That's a wholly inadequate explanation—wholly inadequate for me more than anyone else—but it's the only one I have."

"Did ... they put you in jail?"

"No. It's up to the DA to bring charges. The guy here knew it was an accident. He let me go, but I wish I'd gone to jail. I wish they'd executed me. Some people thought they should have. But they let me go.

"I didn't leave the house for a month. The church tried to be supportive, but people couldn't look at me anymore. I scared them. Some people just thought I was a monster. Others were scared of me because they knew I wasn't. I was a kind, loving father who'd accidentally killed his child. The only thing worse than being a monster is being a daily reminder that horrible things happen for no reason at all.

"Carrie tried to stay with me. She really did. She tried to forgive me. But how can you stay with the man who killed your child? I became the thing I'd done. I couldn't even help her grieve. She lost her child and her husband that day.

"She left me. That was the last time I prayed. I told God I hated him. I came here and burned this place to the ground. They put me in jail, but the church refused to press any charges and then they interceded on my behalf with the DA, again, not to bring criminal charges against me. Their forgiveness just hurt more. I wanted someone to punish me. The church just moved locations. We'd been talking about moving closer to the highway for a while. They saw it as a chance to start over. So they did.

"That was last year. I drifted down to Little Rock. A couple of days ago was the one year … anniversary of the … of me burning down the church. I started thinking. Started drinking."

"And that's when you killed yourself."

"Yes."

"Jesus. I'm sorry, Elliot. I'm so sorry."

I had never told anyone what had happened. At the time of it happening, everyone already knew. Later, when I'd moved away and the story had disappeared with the next day's news cycle, I'd kept my sin to myself. I saw no reason to beg forgiveness from strangers.

"We should go upstairs," I said.

Three faced me as a dim outline in the dark. She turned just a bit, and I could barely see her face.

"Okay," she said.

I followed her to the stairs and up toward the blue-black sky.

I stopped halfway up the step. "Hey."

She turned around at the top. "Yeah."

"I want you to hide in the woods."

"What?"

"I want you to hide in the woods until this is over."

"Why? You don't think I can do this? Hell, I'm the one here knows what she's doing with a shotgun."

"I know. But I want you to hide in the woods. I'm going to get Stan to come down here with me."

"What the hell are you talking about? The plan—"

"I know what the plan was. It doesn't matter. All that matters is that you and Felicia don't get hurt. I want you to hide in the woods. I'll bring Stan down here. I'm starting to get a bad feeling. It this thing goes wrong, you let him go. You don't take a shot at him and you don't go back to the shipment. Forget about the money. You just hide and wait and when he leaves, you get out of Arkansas and don't stop running."

"What if this Felicia broad is in on the deal with Stan?"

"Then you let her go. That's my problem. No matter what happens to me, you take care of yourself."

She sucked in her top lip like she might be mad at me. Then she said, "I'll hide in the woods. But if the shooting starts and I can do anything, you can be damn sure I'll do it."

I knew there would be no use arguing the point. She would do what she would do. "Just take care of yourself," I said.

I started back down the stairs, but she said, "Hey."

Turning back, I said, "Yeah."

"What was your baby's name?"

"Why?"

"I just want to know."

"Her name was Felicia."

The Mercy Seat 20

I had been listening to the dripping of the pipes for less than a minute when I heard a car in the distance. Instinctively, I reached for the small flashlight in my pocket. I stopped myself, steadied my breathing and crouched down.

I expected Stan to park by Three's truck, but the car rolled up right to the burned church. Light spilled down the steps. I'd been sitting in the dark so long, the glare blinded me.

"Goddamn it," I cursed. Why had he come straight to the hole? I had to move. If he left the headlights on and came downstairs, I'd be better off hiding behind the steps.

Crunching blindly across debris, I hurried as quietly as I could, hoping the idle of Stan's engine would cover the sound of my movement downstairs. I dropped next to the charred steps as the engine cut off, followed by the light.

Everything was dark again except for the spots of purple floating across my vision. I shook my head, trying to adjust back to the dark. Outside, a door opened and closed. I heard Felicia call my name, "Elliot!"

I tried to breathe through my nose. The pipes dripped.

Then, behind me. From the darkness of a burned out classroom, all at once: footsteps, a burst of light and two small metallic claps. I spun around, but when I did my right shoulder fell apart. At the same instant there was a jab in my gut. Something exploded in my shoulder and shot down to my fingers, and my shotgun tumbled to the floor. My stomach burst. As I hit the damp, soot-covered floor, my belly started to ooze.

The light shone down on me. Stan knelt by my head, flashlight in one hand and the gun with the long silencer in the other.

His suit was disheveled and black with grime, his red hair dripping with sweat. Ash and sweat streaked his face.

"Come down here," he yelled up the stairs.

At the top of the steps, a flashlight clicked on, and Felicia walked down.

"Stan?" she said.

Stan stood up, holding the gun at his side. "That's right, baby. Come on down here with me and Elliot."

In her left hand, Felicia held her small handgun. She walked nearly to the bottom of the groaning stairs, about two steps up, with the flashlight steady in her hand. "Why'd you bring him down here?" she asked.

"Came down on his own. I was here hiding and he walked over and came downstairs. Guess he had the same idea. I just got here first."

As Stan spoke, I tried to reach the shotgun with my good arm, but he kicked me in the face. My vision burst, and my nose collapsed.

"Behave yourself," he told me.

Through the crisscross of flashlight beams, I could barely make out Felicia's face. She didn't look scared.

"Did you find out where the truck is?" she asked.

Stan said, "Elliot, tell Felicia where the truck is."

In a bloody mumble I told them where I'd parked it.

Felicia's face flickered in and out of focus just over the flare from her flashlight, and it seemed like a different face each time it came back in focus. Sad. Defiant. Guilty. Greedy.

Stan knelt beside me. "She betrayed you for the money. I guess you put that together by now."

I didn't say anything. Nothing to say. Let them all go. Felicia could go on her way and live the life she'd chosen. Three could get away.

Stan said, "Felicia, you want to say anything to Elliot here?"

"Stop it, Stan. There's no need to torture him."

"I'm serious. The man only has a couple of minutes left to live. Do you want his last thoughts to be bad ones about you?"

She lowered her flashlight and stood half-obscured in darkness and half-revealed in pale light from above.

"Why is he smiling?"

"Elliot," Stan said, "she wants to know why you're smiling." Stan leaned down close to me, with the flashlight in my face, his sweat dripping on me. "I know why. It's because you get to be a martyr. That it, Elliot? You get to redeem yourself by saving Felicia and the Thickroot girl?"

Felicia took another step down. "What do you mean?"

"I mean Elliot doesn't care that he's dying because he sees his dying as a way to atone for his sins." Stan chewed the inside of his cheek. "Right?"

Felicia's voice quivered as she said, "I'm sorry, Elliot. I really—a"

Stan shot her in the chest as she was speaking, and she jerked backward and hit the wall. Her feet slipped forward, and she tumbled down the last step and shot the concrete floor. Stan rose up, his gun outstretched, but Felicia was dead.

He sighed heavily through his nose. He shone the light down in my face. "You still with me, Elliot?"

I tried to say something, but it came out in tangle of blood and spit.

"What?" he said.

"Felicia."

"She's better off," Stan said. "You know, up until the point you called me I had every intention of letting her live. But when you said you wanted to meet here, of all places, then it clicked. The preacher that killed his baby and burned down his church.

"Then I knew why it had never been about the money with you. It was about redemption this whole time. You wanted to save Felicia."

Light pierced my eyes like I was on an examination table.

"Why you shoot her?" I asked weakly.

"Because of you," he said. "You killed your baby, Elliot. Even I couldn't bring myself to eat my lunch while my only child boiled to death in the parking lot. But I can deny you your redemption. What better way to ensure the glory of my own salvation than to deny you yours?"

Everything disappeared for a moment. Then it came back.

"I can't … move," I managed to say.

"You're going to have to. You have to go up those steps where your little friend is waiting. She heard Felicia's gun, and now I bet she's taking a real good aim at the top of these stairs."

"Don't hurt her," I said.

"Why not?"

"Please."

"'Please' isn't a reason, Elliot. That's what people like you never understand."

"She's innocent."

"So was your child, Elliot."

I spit out blood. My head floated, tethered only tenuously to my neck. My limbs buzzed, heavy and numb.

"Please," I said.

"Please again," Stan grunted. He pulled my right arm and I felt nothing. He yanked me up and pushed me against the wall.

"Listen to me," he said. "I like you. I did from the start. I told Thickroot to kill you quick, but he was incompetent, and you worked your way out of that. Good for you. You bought yourself another few hours. But now here you are, and you are going up those stairs."

I didn't try to talk.

He said, "You know why you're going up those stairs? Because if you don't, I'll go out there and get her. I'll bring her down here, and I'll gut her like a deer." He slapped my face. "And you'll watch every bit of it."

"Icanbarelymove."

"You can move. You wanted to die, didn't you? Well, here you go. Go up there, take the kid's bullets. If you're lucky, she's run off already. If not, I promise you I'll make it quick like Felicia. She won't suffer."

I nodded. Stan pushed me closer to the steps. As I tried to walk, my legs were sticky with blood from my belly. Felicia lay sprawled across the steps with her blue eyes open and her head bent to the side as if she were incredulous. The gun had kicked out of her hand when it fired and lay near her foot. I touched the black star on her wrist.

Stan pushed me up the first step. "This is it," he said. "It's time to go explain yourself to God."

I climbed the steps like a man climbing the gallows. I wasn't afraid of Three shooting me. I assumed she would and then that would be the end of me. I didn't worry about that. I worried about whether or not she could get away before Stan got to her. And if she did, would she have the sense to keep running? To flee Arkansas and Stan the Man?

"Keep going," Stan said.

My shoes were wet now. I heard it more than felt it. I didn't know if it was blood or sweat. All I could feel was my life seeping out my stomach as I tried to pull air into my lungs.

The first weak rays of morning shone down on me as I stumbled up the steps, but I could see the moon, faint and bruised, shaking in the sky as I climbed toward it. I would be dead in a moment ... *I'll never see Felicia again ... never apologize to her for the pain I caused her ... in our marriage*

... and ... no, Carrie ... and the day I asked Carrie to be my wife ... Carrie ... my baby's pale body falling away from me into the darkness ... Three falling away from me ...

go, stan said

the moon trembled like a dying woman's last words, and i threw myself backward onto stan, and we shattered the stairs like a wrecking ball, splintering wood and nails and brick, and stan the man snapped beneath me when we smashed into the concrete floor and the world collapsed on top of us

the sky hurried over me i tried to move but i couldn't feel anything to move

be still she said we're going to the hospital

treetops the rush of air through a window

i tried to speak but i had no voice no mouth

just stay with me she said that was the last thing i heard her say

just stay with me

†

About the Author

Jake Hinkson is the author of several books—including the novels *Hell On Church Street*, *The Posthumous Man* and *The Big Ugly*, the short story collection *The Deepening Shade*, and the essay collection *The Blind Alley: Exploring Film Noir's Forgotten Corners*. Born in Arkansas and raised in the Ozarks, he currently lives in Chicago. His books *Hell On Church Street* and *The Posthumous Man* have been translated into French by èditions Gallmeister.

For more, visit JakeHinkson.com and
TheNightEditor.blogspot.com.

Also by JAKE HINKSON

from BEAT to a PULP books
www.beattoapulp.com

THE BIG UGLY — Ellie Bennett is an ex-corrections officer who has just served a year inside Eastgate Penitentiary for assaulting a prisoner. She's only been out for a day when she accepts a strange job offer from the head of a Christian political advocacy group. He wants her to track down a missing ex-con named Alexis. Although no one knows where Alexis has gone, it seems like everyone in Arkansas is looking for her-from a rich televangelist running for Congress to the governor's dirty tricks man. When Bennett finds the troubled young woman, she has to decide whether to hand her over to the highest bidder or help her escape from the most powerful men in the state.

Keep an eye on Jake Hinkson. He's taking the notion of the sacred and the profane to an entirely new level in noir.   **—Lou Boxer**
co-founder of NoirCon

* * *

Hinkson is a master at creating, not characters, but people—and then putting them through hell.   **—Steve Weddle**
author of *Country Hardball*

* * *

Jake Hinkson is a thunderhead on the horizon of crime fiction ... take shelter and prepare for nasty weather.   **—Jedidiah Ayres**
author of *Peckerwood*

Made in the USA
Charleston, SC
25 February 2016